Culver's Cove

THE TRAPICHE EMERALD

BY D. M. GLOVER

Book design by Karina Granda
Cave photo copyright © Cavan Images/Offset
Light image copyright © Net Vector/shutterstock.com
Dog silhouette copyright © Design_Lands/shutterstock.com

Paperback ISBN: 978-1-966227-00-7
eBook ISBN: 978-1-966227-01-4

In honor of our forefathers and the men and women
who died fighting for America's freedoms.

To America's heroes in the elite fighting forces of the
Army / Navy / Air Force / Marines

This book is dedicated with sincere gratitude.

—And—

In loving memory of
William Arthur Culver, Jr.
November 7, 1962 ~ April 18, 2018
U.S. Navy Petty Officer Third Class

"Time and space are modes by which we think
and not conditions by which we live."
—ALBERT EINSTEIN

⭐ CHAPTER ONE ⭐

"Stop slamming that door!" Heath's mom, Hailey, yelled from the kitchen. The screen door made a loud sound that resembled a shotgun being fired and it made her jump every time. Heath thought it was kinda funny.

Heath, an eleven-year-old boy with brown hair, brown eyes, and a memory like an elephant yelled from the living room, "Sorry Mom, I forgot." As he walked into the kitchen, he was overcome with the smell of cinnamon buns that she made for him this morning.

Hadden, his little brother, was sitting at the table finishing his cereal. He was two years younger than Heath and looked completely different with his blue eyes and sandy blond hair. Hadden looked just like his mom except for the curl in his hair, which always made it seem messy. Another difference between Hadden and his mom was that Hadden was pigeon-toed, which made him trip a lot. Heath, on the other hand, was a mini-me of his dad, Logan.

"Hey goofball, are you almost done?" Heath asked. He was anxious to get started on the day. It was the first day of summer vacation and he didn't want to waste a minute of it.

"Yup, whatcha wanna do?" Hadden asked after swallowing another bite of his second bowl of cereal. Hadden was a kid who could eat a lot and talk a lot. He would talk so much sometimes that Heath began calling him Sir Talks A-Lot.

"I was thinking of going fishing and then swimming at Culver's Cove."

"Oh no you're not!" his mom exclaimed. "I don't want you two going there without any supervision."

"See what you did, doofus? You and your drowning last year scared her," Hadden said with a mouth full of cereal.

Heath thought back to last year when he was swimming in the lake at Culver's Cove. He saw Hadden on the beach and had a great idea. He went underwater and when he came back up he threw his arms around and splashed like he was drowning. He knew not to make any noise because he had recently learned that when people drown, they don't have enough time to make any noise, they pretty much panic. Hadden panicked and yelled, "Heath's drowning! Help 'em, Dad! Save 'em!"

Logan didn't waste any time and ran into the lake to save his son. By the time he dove in and came back up for air, he noticed that Heath was floating on his back, doing a backstroke back to shore. Logan stayed there until Heath reached him, and with one eyebrow raised he said, "Sooo, I take it you don't need any help."

Heath kept his backstroke going and gave his dad a devilish smile that confirmed that he was just teasing his little brother once again. Logan lunged toward Heath in an attempt to grab him by the leg as he swam by. Heath dodged his dad's playful attack and swam away. Logan swam after him and they began to race back to shore, but when he caught up to Heath he slowed down to let him win.

"Yes, it did scare me and I don't care how well you swim. You are not going there alone," Heath's mom stated.

"Well, can we go fishing there then?"

Hailey looked at her eldest and thought for a moment. "Mmm, I don't think so, honey. I know you too well and you will end up swimming anyway."

"No, we won't, I promise," Heath said as he raised his right hand in sincerity.

Hailey continued to look at her son and sighed. She knew that Heath understood the importance of a promise. However, she was not going to take any chances. "No, I'm sorry, honey. I don't like you and Hadden swimming without adult supervision. Anything can happen."

Heath plopped down at the kitchen table across from Hadden and sulked with disappointment. "Well, now what are we supposed to do?"

"You can go to Danny's house and play outside," his mom suggested. "He has that new trampoline."

Heath shook his head. "Danny went with his mom and sister to his aunt's today so he probably won't be home until dinner time. All the kids in the neighborhood are going somewhere except us. If they were still around we could have a football game or something but now all I can do is find something to do with Hadden." Then he sat up with a great idea. "Ooh, can we-"

Hailey already knew what his next words were going to be and said a quick, "No, you aren't playing video games," cutting Heath off in mid-sentence. "You both are going outside and playing in this beautiful weather before it gets too hot and then maybe you can play your video games."

Heath sat back and slumped in his chair again and sighed.

Hadden slurped the last of what was left in the cereal bowl and dropped it in the sink. Heath pushed his chair out and their border collie, Zeus, quickly got up to check out the floor for anything that may have fallen before following the boys out. Once in the living room, Heath pulled on Hadden's shirt sleeve and pulled him closer so he could whisper into his ear. "Hey, we can still go fishing. We just won't tell Mom. She didn't say no to fishing and I just promised we wouldn't go swimming, not fishing. Whadda ya think?"

Hadden, always the optimist, said, "Okay, and I'm gonna catch Old Lucky today," as he slapped Heath on the arm.

Old Lucky was a striped bass that seemed to grow bigger and bigger each year and was too smart to get caught. Mr. Peterson, their friend Danny's father, said he caught him two years ago but he got away. Everyone in town hoped to catch Old Lucky.

Heath opened the screen door and Zeus ran out first. Hadden followed behind, making sure not to slam the door. The boys sat on the top step of the porch with their elbows on their knees and their chins in the palms of their hands.

Heath thought, *We can sneak around to the back of the house to get the fishing poles from the garage, but the only bad thing about that is Mom is in the kitchen and can see us if she looks out the window.* "Okay, how's this?" he said under his breath to Hadden. "You sneak down the driveway, go around back, and put one of the patio chairs below the kitchen window. Climb up and peek in to see if Mom's still in the kitchen."

"Why do I have to do it? It's your idea, you do it."

"'Cuz you're smaller than me so it's easier for you to jump on the chair and peek in the window without being seen."

Hadden's brow lifted as he thought about that. "I'm not buying it, but I am better at sneaking around than you are because I'm like a ninja," he said as he did his ninja moves. "Sneaky, stealthy, and adorable, so I'll do it."

Heath smiled and patted Hadden on the back. "You are so right, little brother."

"Okay, I'll look in the corner window and if she's not in the kitchen I'll wave to ya like this." Hadden held his hand up and moved it side to side.

"Okay, let's rock, let's roll, let's achieve our goal!" Heath said as he clapped his hands.

Hadden bent over and began skulking down the driveway towards the backyard. He picked up a patio chair and placed it against the house underneath the corner window. He quietly crept up onto the chair and looked in the window. He saw his mom walking into the living room and then held the window frame to brace himself in order to wave to Heath with his free hand when suddenly he fell off the chair. The chair hit the cement patio and made a loud bang. He waited a moment and when he didn't hear his mom coming, he got back up on the chair to double check on her whereabouts. He got off the chair this time and waved to Heath that the coast was still clear and ran to the garage.

Hadden flipped the light switch on and Heath panicked that his mom would know that they were in the garage. He imagined flipping the light off before he yelled, "Turn that off, ya dork! What if Mom sees the light on?" but before Hadden turned the switch off, the lights went out by themselves.

"If I'm a dork, you're a double dork. Wait, I didn't turn 'em off yet," Hadden replied as he flipped the light switch off. His eyes adjusted to the darkness rather quickly with the help of the windows on the garage door. He flipped the switch on once more just to be sure that the lights still worked. When they went on, he immediately flipped it off.

"Whatcha do that for?" Heath asked.

"I just wanted to be sure that the lights still worked cuz I didn't turn 'em off before and they just went off by themselves," Hadden explained.

"Oh, okay." Heath thought it was weird but didn't think anything more about it.

They already knew where the fishing equipment was. They went fishing all the time with their dad but since he was working today they had to go without him. "You grab the tackle box and I'll get the poles," said Heath.

The boys grabbed their fishing equipment and headed out of the garage.

"Wait," Hadden said, grabbing Heath's shoulder to hold him back. "Look in the kitchen windows first and see if Mom went back into the kitchen."

Heath opened the garage door a crack and peeked through the opening. He had a direct line of vision to the kitchen window from here. "No. Let's go, Joe!"

Heath led the way. He hunched over and crept down the driveway but forgot to bring the fishing poles below the window. If his mom had been in the living room, she would have seen two fishing poles walking by.

Hadden quietly closed the garage door and ran up to the front of the house. Knowing they were almost in the clear,

Hadden said, "Now it's your turn to go and peek in the front of the house to see if Mom is in the living room. If she isn't, then we can run across the driveway and run behind the bushes in the Petersons' yard."

Heath rolled his eyes and handed the poles to Hadden. "Watch and learn, little brother. Watch and learn." Heath went to the front of the steps and quietly crawled up to the porch. The family cat, Peaches, was lying on the chair underneath the window and gave him a once over as he crawled beneath the living room window. As Heath slowly rose to stand on the left side of the window, he slid his back against the house and placed his thumb and his pointer finger out on his right hand and cupped it in his left pretending he had a gun in his hands like James Bond. He kept his arms bent up against his chest ready to aim when necessary. James Bond would most likely use one eye to peer into the window so he attempted this move. Heath tried to close his left eye, but both eyes closed. He tried again to keep his right eye open while he closed his left. He just couldn't do it. Heath closed his right eye instead and tilted his head to the right until he could see inside with his left eye.

Suddenly, Zeus jumped up onto the chair where Peaches was sitting. Peaches jumped down with a screech, scratching the floor as she scurried off. Both Heath and Zeus were now looking in the same window. If Hailey had been looking out of the window, she would have seen Zeus in the center of the window with his tongue hanging out of his mouth. On Zeus's left was the top of Heath's head looking in sideways, with one eye opened and one eye closed.

Heath held his breath for a few seconds in fear because of all the noise Zeus had caused. When he knew the coast was clear, Heath quietly tiptoed across the porch.

Zeus jumped off the chair, making it hit the house, and ran down the steps.

Once Heath made it down to the last step, he said, "Let's go!" Hadden, Heath, and Zeus ran across the driveway and hid behind the bushes in the Petersons' yard.

There, the boys bent over with their hands on their knees and took a breath.

"Ah man, we made it!" Heath said with excitement.

They had to take a moment to catch their breath and let their heartbeats slow down a bit. Sneaking around was nerve-racking.

Hadden turned around to begin their journey to Culver's Cove when he spotted Mr. Peterson. He grabbed Heath's shirt and pointed to where Mr. Peterson was squatting down with his back toward them, petting Zeus. Mr. Peterson was pulling weeds in his flower beds when Zeus ran over to greet him.

Heath shrugged. "Oh, well. What are we gonna do about it now? Let's just hope that he doesn't talk to Mom today and tell her about the fishing poles."

As they walked towards their neighbor, both boys said in unison, "Hi, Mr. Peterson." Hadden swung his arm over to connect with Heath's chest with the back of his hand while he said, "Jinx."

Mr. Peterson looked up to greet them. "Well, hello boys. I figured you two wouldn't be far behind when Zeus came running up to me." He stood up. "I see you're going fishing."

Hadden piped up. "Yeah, I'm gonna catch Old Lucky. If it's not today, it will be this summer. I can feel it in my bones, like Mom always says, I got a vibe about it," he said with a smile.

Mr. Peterson laughed. "Well, good luck. If either of you does catch him, be sure to take a picture. I'd love to see how big Old Lucky got."

"I will," they both replied.

This time Heath tapped Hadden's shoulder with the back of his hand as he said, "Jinx."

"Well, have fun. Too bad Danny isn't here. I bet he'd love to go fishing with you," Mr. Peterson said as he knelt down to get back to his gardening.

"Yeah, maybe next time. Have a nice day, Mr. Peterson," Heath said as he waved goodbye.

Heath and Hadden walked down the street hoping not to run into anyone else. When you live in a town like Free-hold, everyone knows everyone and everyone talks. Heath was also worried about running into Conor Kingsley. Conor was a year older than Heath and a big bully that terrorized anyone he could. Heath thought about the other day when he and Hadden went to Jersey Freeze to get ice cream cones after school. Conor walked in and Heath's stomach churned and an overwhelming feeling of dread took hold.

"Hey it's Heath the Freak and the pigeon-toed geek." Conor yelled toward Heath and Hadden.

Heath was not one to fight. Having a fight with Hadden was different; he cared about his little brother, even though he would never admit to it. When it came to anyone else, he didn't want to be bothered because their presence wasn't worth his time. Heath turned to Hadden and whispered, "Don't pay any attention to him, let's go."

Hadden, on the other hand, was the opposite. He might be a little smaller than Heath but he was feisty, fearless, and faithful. "No way!" he said to Heath. He turned to look at Conor and said, "I was wondering what that stink was when the door opened."

Conor blocked the exit they were heading to. "Where do you think you're going? I'll take that ice cream cone, thank you very much," he said as he reached for Hadden's ice cream cone.

"In your dreams, ya little inseam," Hadden said as he pulled his cone back closer to him to protect the goods.

Heath already knew of the wooden sign hanging above the door saying "Thanks, Come Again" and he imagined it falling on top of Conor's head. Conor never got the chance to grab Hadden's ice cream cone. When it hit Conor on the head, Conor stood there in utter shock for a few seconds, giving Heath time to grab Hadden by the shirt and scoot through the door. "Come on, let's go."

"Whoa, can you believe that? That was awesome," Hadden said as he was being dragged through the door by the back of his shirt. "What perfect timing was that!"

"Yeah, let's just go home now, I don't want to sit here and run into Conor again," he said with a frown.

Hadden was licking his cone, trying to keep up with the drips of melting ice cream. "Yeah, he will probably blame us somehow for that sign falling on his head."

As they walked to Culver's Cove, Heath wondered if there was any truth to what Conor called him. His mom always said that you should listen to your gut and his gut was saying there's something different about him lately. He thought it was weird how he imagined the sign falling on Conor and it happened just the way that he thought it. *Oh wow, I forgot about yesterday!*

Since yesterday was the last day of school, the class sat in the cafeteria for snacks. Bobby was sitting directly across from Heath and suddenly he had a look of fear on his face.

"What's wrong?" Heath asked as he turned to look in the direction Bobby was looking in.

"Conor just walked in," Bobby replied.

Heath looked toward Conor and cringed. "He got to me and Hadden in Jersey Freeze the other day. He wouldn't let us out the door unless Hadden gave him his ice cream cone."

"Oh man, that stinks. What happened?"

Heath said, "Nothing much happened. Conor went to grab Hadden's cone and the sign above the door fell on his head."

"Oh dude, you're lucky. He got me last week on my way home from school. He ran up from behind me and pulled my back pack so I went falling down in the bushes." Bobby turned around slightly and showed Heath the back of his arm. "See, I still have the scratches from it."

"Oh man. Last week he tripped Maggie in the hall. She was carrying a bunch of books and when he tripped her, the books went flying in every direction, papers took off down the hall, and Maggie was flat on her face. People laughed and when she got up to get her things, I was the only one to help her. Her face was so red. I felt bad for her," Heath said as he glanced behind again to see what Conor was up to. "Don't look over there and maybe he won't notice us." He took another drink from his juice box trying to look like he didn't have a care in the world or noticed Conor at all.

"I can't help it. I feel like I have to watch his every move now when I know he's around. It looks like he's going to bother Billy. We might be safe for today."

"Yeah, but the day still has a lot left of it," Heath said as he turned around and saw that Conor was sneaking up on Billy and about to steal his bag of Doritos. When Heath saw what was about to happen, his imagination took over. He imagined the straw that was sticking out of Billy's juice box slowly turning towards Conor and spewing juice out all over him.

Conor snuck up to Billy and snatched the bag of Doritos from him and as he went to grab the juice box, the juice suddenly started spurting out from the straw before Conor could even touch it. It sprayed directly at his pants, making it look like he peed himself, which made him more mad than embarrassed. Even though Billy's hand was nowhere near the box, Conor yelled, "I know you did that on purpose, you little twerp." Then he leaned closer to Billy and whispered something in his ear. He stood up and threw the bag of Doritos at the boy and stormed off.

Billy was the only one that witnessed what happened, but wasn't sure what actually happened. The straw moved all by itself and shot at Conor's pants. No one was anywhere near it and he knew he didn't touch it. If anyone else had seen what truly happened, no one acknowledged it. Billy sat there in stunned silence trying to figure out what just took place and how.

Heath thought about this morning with the lights in the garage. *Maybe Conor is right, maybe I am a freak.* As Hadden was talking about his last day of school, Heath was deep in his thoughts. He was so sure that something was happening with him that he wanted to do an experiment. As they passed the next house, Heath saw a child's tricycle in the yard. He imagined it moving forward and suddenly it lurched forward. "Oh my God!" Heath shouted.

"What? Is it Conor the cone head?" Hadden wanted to know.

"That tricycle over there moved cuz…" Heath stopped in mid-sentence because he didn't want Hadden thinking he was crazy.

"Cuz why?" Hadden asked.

"Never mind." Heath changed the subject. "It must have been my imagination."

When they got home they sat on the front porch with their elbows on their knees and their faces in the palms of their hands, wondering what to do next. Out of the corner of Heath's eye he spotted their neighbor, Danny, through the bushes that lined the driveway. Heath thought he'd experiment with this mind control stuff some more. He noticed the black hose that his mom had used earlier that day was stretched out along the edge of the driveway. Since it was black, it blended in with the mulch. It ran along the driveway and as it got closer to the end of the driveway, it rose up a bit, just enough to make Danny trip if he didn't see it. Heath imagined the hose moving and straightening itself out. Imagine Heath's surprise when he watched as the hose stretched out and by the time Danny reached the hose, it was flat so he didn't trip over it. This mind control stuff was beginning to weigh heavy on him, especially since he always felt a little different from everyone else to begin with. Heath didn't know what to think about it anymore so he decided to just stop thinking about it, period.

★ CHAPTER TWO ★

ZEUS LED THE WAY THROUGH THE WOODS ON THE WELL-worn path. It came to an end at a clearing that looked like a little piece of paradise. The entire town knew that the lake was bought by William Culver, Jr. about a century ago. When you came out of the woods, on the left was a good size beach and on the right, the beach narrowed to twenty feet wide. The right side of the lake was perfect for fishing and the left side was perfect for sunbathers and swimmers.

The boys knew they were getting close to the beach because the sun shined brighter as they made their way through the woods. When they came to the clearing, they noticed across the lake on the left were three people sunbathing, two people swimming, and kids making sand castles. Out of habit, Hadden started to head to the left of the lake with Zeus running the usual twenty feet ahead of him.

"Wait, we've always gone over there," Heath shouted. "Let's go to the other side."

Hadden stopped, saluted, and he made an about turn. "Okie dokie smokie."

Zeus looked back and saw the boys heading in the other direction, then he took off running to catch up.

When they made it to the narrow side of the lake Hadden opened the tackle box and began looking for a hook to use.

Zeus was sniffing around everywhere. With all the new scents to smell, Hadden figured he was in heaven.

Heath was just standing there with a fishing pole in each hand, staring into the woods.

Hadden looked up at him. "Come on. What are you waiting for, a written invitation?" He paused and scribbled in the air as if he were holding a pen and said, "Here, consider it written," as he put his arm out as if he were handing him a piece of paper.

Heath said, "I was just thinking. We always come here to the lake with Mom and Dad and we have never walked through the woods before. You wanna check it out?"

Hadden looked towards the woods. It was dense and overgrown and looked like no one had gone through these woods in a very long time. He stood up and raised his eyebrows with excitement. "Yeah, man. That's a great idea," he said as he put the hook back into the tackle box and closed the lid.

Heath leaned the fishing poles up against a tree. "Let's just leave our fishing stuff here."

Hadden placed the tackle box next to the poles.

They both looked at each other. "Ready Freddie?" Heath asked.

"Yupper, let's go, Joe." Hadden waved his arm in the direction that they were to go and said, "After you, sir."

Heath went first as they headed into the woods. On this side of the lake, the woods were overgrown with weeds, trees, and bushes, and the ground was covered in leaves from previous autumns. Heath pushed the brush out of his way as he made his way through. One branch swung back and hit Hadden in the chest.

"Hey, nimrod! Knock it off!" he screamed.

"Don't stand so close, Dingleberry Finn," Heath said looking back as he continued on. Then he spotted what looked like an old path where the weeds weren't as thick.

Even Zeus was struggling to make it through the dense foliage, so Heath turned onto the path where it was not so bad.

Hadden began telling Heath about how Suzie Stevens kissed him at recess yesterday, but Heath wasn't really listening to him. He'd gotten so used to his brother's incessant chatter that he learned to tune him out. Although he did hear Hadden yell, "Ouch. You stupid jerk," to a branch that caught onto his shirt. Hadden yanked his shirt off the branch and carefully plucked off the round, prickly cocklebur seeds that stuck to him.

Hadden followed in the footsteps of his older brother trying to avoid getting hit by any more branches or stabbed by any more cocklebur seeds. They had been hiking for fifteen minutes before Hadden said in a grumpy tone, "Hey, I'm tired of this, let's go back. There's nothing out here."

"Wouldn't it be cool if we found the old Culver house?" Heath replied, ignoring his brother's cries. Maybe Mr. Culver's ghost is in there." Heath smiled as he turned back to see Hadden's reaction. Mr. Culver abandoned the original old house when he built his new home on the opposite side of the property. The old house had been abandoned and hidden in the woods ever since. People said it was haunted.

"If Mr. Culver's ghost is walking around, you won't see anything of me except my dust," Hadden said in a serious tone.

Heath could see it getting brighter and knew that they were coming to the end of the woods. The first thing that he saw was an incline where the ground began to rise up on what appeared to be a black wall. The wall was about fifteen feet high and made from layers of black slate rock. On top of it was grass and ivy hanging down. Heath thought it was actually very pretty. "Whoa. Check it out," Heath said in amazement.

Hadden brought up the rear, tripping into Heath. Heath didn't say anything about him knocking into him so Hadden knew something awesome was there. He looked ahead at what Heath was so amazed about. He was a bit disappointed by the sight. "We made it all the way to the end of the woods for this?" Hadden exclaimed.

"This can't just end here. There is supposed to be a big ole house somewhere on this property. If we walk up the hill over there–," Heath pointed over to the left where the hill began–. "We can look down and maybe see where it is from the top of this wall."

Hadden noticed that Zeus wasn't anywhere in sight. He began yelling, "Zeus, here boy!" and whistled for him.

Heath figured the dog was just roaming around the woods since there was so much to see. He did get a little worried about him though. Zeus always came when he was called. "Weren't you keeping an eye on him?"

"Yeah, I had the same eye on 'em as you did," Hadden replied.

Heath rolled his eyes and said, "I know he didn't go up the hill because we would have seen him. Let's go this way and look."

Hadden shook his head feeling that this was a bad idea, but what else were they supposed to do? He made sure to keep beside the rock wall so it would be easy to find their way back.

Heath turned around to Hadden. "Maybe Zeus found the old Culver house? Maybe this path leads there." As soon as Heath finished the words, he saw Zeus come running out of an opening in the wall they were following. Heath stopped abruptly. "Look! It's a cave! We found a hidden cave!" he said with excitement. Zeus ran right back into the cave, so he thought that it must be safe. "Let's check it out!"

Hadden leaned around the side of the cave to take a peek into the opening. "Ah, nnnope. Nuh uh. I'm not going in there. No way Jose," he said matter-of-factly. "Are you crazy? It's dark in there!"

"Once your eyes get used to it you'll be able to see better, just like in the garage," Heath insisted.

Hadden still didn't like the idea. He didn't have a fear of most things, but things were different when it came to a dark, mysterious cave that may have a man-eating bear. Plus, the only thing Hadden did fear was the dark. "How do you know that we won't run into a bear or something?"

Heath stood there scratching his head for a second as he considered the possibility. "Nah, I've watched a lot of nature shows about animals and stuff and if a bear lived in there, he left already. They only sleep in the winter and they fatten up in the summertime."

"Yeah, it'll fatten up on me!"

Heath shook his head. "If a bear comes, I'll jump out in front of you so he eats me first. Okay?" he said sarcastically.

"No you won't, you'll run and leave me behind so he eats me. I came downstairs the other night when Dad was watching something on TV about a bear killing a man, tore him to pieces, and ate 'em!" Hadden exclaimed.

Heath really wanted to explore the cave and was trying to figure out what to say to Hadden to make him feel better about it. "Hey, you know what? I am so sure that there isn't a bear in this cave that I will go in and show you myself." Heath walked in about ten feet and stopped to let his eyes adjust a bit. He turned to Hadden. "See, there's nothing in here. And besides, Zeus checked everything out already so it's definitely safe."

Hadden still didn't like the thought of going into that dark hole, but he knew Heath would tease him if he didn't go in. "Okay, fine, but you go first. If a bear is going to eat us or a bat flies into us they'll get you first," he said sarcastically as he slowly entered the cave.

The cave entrance was only about eight feet wide, then inside it opened to about twenty feet wide and ten feet high. The walls were made of charcoal colored stone and the floor was dry powdery light-gray dirt. A three-foot circular hole in the ceiling allowed a little sunlight into the cave, making it easier to see.

Zeus was still sniffing away at every spot he could find.

Heath had an overabundance of curiosity and just had to explore the rest of this cave, but he didn't want to do it all by himself. If he was going down, he didn't want to go down alone.

Hadden wasn't happy about going any farther into the cave but he wasn't going to act like a scaredy cat.

Heath explained, "See, once your eyes get used to the dark then we can go a little farther down. The hole in the ceiling helps to make it a little brighter in here too." He could tell that Hadden was pretty scared because Sir Talks A-Lot wasn't talking a lot.

Hadden figured since Zeus wasn't barking, it must be safe, "Okay, just a little farther."

Heath took ten steps deeper into the cave and noticed that a section on the right side of the wall shined and looked smoother than the rest of the wall. He moved a few steps closer.

Hadden asked, "What are you doing?"

"Uh, I'm checking out this wall." On the right side of the cave he rubbed his hand across the wall, feeling it. "It... I dunno. It's shiny and very smooth compared to the rest of the cave. It's weird." Heath slid his hand down the hard steel-gray section of the wall as he walked along, enjoying the cool smoothness. A few spots caught the sunlight that came in, giving it the look of shining silver. After about fifteen feet, it got rough and black again. Heath looked at the opposite wall and it was the same black slate the entire length of the cave.

Hadden had enough. "I think this is good enough, let's go. What if a bear comes back for something?"

As he continued down along the wall another few feet Heath said, "I told you that bears are out of hibernation now. Don't worry about bears!"

"Well, what if it came back in for a nap?" Hadden challenged.

Heath rolled his eyes and turned to look at Hadden. "I think this cave goes down a lot farther. Come on."

"Oooh heck no! And that's with a capital H!"

Even though Zeus was with them, Heath really didn't want to go alone.

Zeus had finished sniffing around and just sat there looking at his boys. He was probably wondering what they were thinking of doing.

Heath could usually figure out a way to compromise with Hadden. "Okay, let's just sit here for a few minutes and think about this. Our eyes will adjust to the dark again and then we can see better. Then we can go check out the rest of the cave."

"You think that I'm being a scaredy cat, but I'm not, I'm being smart. You don't know what's down there. Maybe a snake is curled up and attacks us or bats come flying out and get stuck in our hair."

Heath laughed and slid down the wall of the cave to sit. "Yeah, with that mess on your head, a few of 'em might get stuck."

Hadden sat down to sit next to Heath while Zeus walked over to lie next to Hadden.

"I really want to see where it ends. Nothing will probably happen." Heath insisted.

"What do you mean nothing will PROBABLY happen?"

"Oh, don't worry," Heath said, looking back down the tunnel. "I mean it WON'T happen. Period."

Hadden was not playing around. "We can come back with a flashlight and see a lot better," he suggested. "Then we can see where this thing goes."

Heath didn't want to go all the way back home, sneak around again, and then come all the way back here. As he was thinking of his next move, he caught something out of the corner of his eye. There was something on the ground a few feet away from where he was just previously standing. "Hey, what's that?" He got up and walked over to pick up the object. It was partially buried in the dirt. It was a round green gemstone about 1 ½" round and ¼" thick. In the center was a black circle that had six black spokes extending out to divide the gemstone into six green equal pieces. He raised it in Hadden's direction for him to see. "Whoa, look at this! It looks like a flower. I wonder where it came from? I'm gonna take it home to Mom."

Hadden was as clueless as Heath was and shrugged. "I dunno. Let me see it."

After Heath studied it a bit, he handed the stone over to Hadden to check out. Hadden wasn't worried about the dark anymore. He was too fascinated with the gemstone. Even though there wasn't a tremendous amount of light in the cave, he was able to hold it from the sides and the light from the ceiling hit it, making the green in the stone look extraordinarily beautiful.

"Okay, that's enough. Let me have it," Heath said as he reached for the gemstone. But Hadden closed the stone inside his right fist and pulled his hand back. Heath attempted to grab it again. "Let me have it, ya dork. I found it and don't want to lose it."

Hadden hated it when Heath was very demanding and not very polite when he wanted something from him. "I'm not done lookin' at it," he said sarcastically.

If Hadden drops this stone it will fall into this powdery dirt and we may never find it again. Heath let Hadden look at the gemstone for another minute. "Okay, you looked long enough. Now let me have it."

"Well, what's the magic word?" Hadden said with a sly smile.

That just annoyed Heath and he lunged for his brother as he said, "I'll magic word ya."

Hadden once again pulled his arm back, keeping the stone in his possession. He pushed Heath away and Heath fell backward.

Heath yelled as he got up and swatted the dirt off his bottom. "Let me have it! I found it!"

Zeus knew well enough to get up and move out of the way when these two went at it.

Hadden held the gemstone tightly in his right fist. "You

can have it back when you say the magic word."

Heath noticed a sort of glow emanating out of Hadden's fist. "Whoa, it's starting to glow!" he exclaimed.

"Yeah, sure, you just want me to look so you can say made you look and snatch it from me. I'm not falling for it."

"No, dude, really, it's glowing. Let me see it." He was now desperate to have it back, to find out more about it and why it was glowing. He tried using his mind powers to make Hadden drop it, but it didn't work. He lunged for Hadden's hand but Hadden was too fast and moved before he could grab it.

Once again Hadden demanded with a sly smile, "What's the magic word?"

That just infuriated Heath and he wasn't willing to negotiate now. Heath charged and jumped on Hadden, knocking them both to the ground. They rolled back and forth as they wrestled with each other in the powdery dirt. They rolled directly toward the wall on the left side of the cave. As they hit the wall they came to a stop, but then suddenly the wall gave way and they continued to roll.

They stopped fighting when they felt something a little strange. They both had sensed something had gone through their bodies for a split second. They let go of each other and lay there in the grass looking up at the trees and the beautiful blue sky.

★ CHAPTER THREE ★

HADDEN LOOKED AROUND. THEY WERE SOMEHOW BACK out in the woods again. He saw the stone wall outside of the cave, but the trees looked different and there was a lot more grass and hardly any weeds. The air even had a different scent to it. With his eyebrow raised he said, "Are you seeing this or am I going crazy?"

Heath just nodded.

"Yeah, you see it or yeah, I'm going crazy?" Hadden stood up and wiped off his shorts and tee shirt. "How did we get here? What the heck happened?"

Still too stunned to speak, Heath just shrugged. When he was able to move he stood up. He didn't even bother wiping off the dirt.

"I don't know what happened but let's get outta here," Hadden said. "This is really weird."

Heath thought that was the best idea his brother ever had. The shock was gone and asked, "But where's Zeus?" as he looked around. They began calling for the dog, but he didn't come running. "What happened? I'm worried about Zeus."

Hadden was worried too, but to reassure Heath he said, "Maybe he just went home. Maybe he heard something that sounded like a gun fire or something and it scared him. They have really good hearing."

"Yeah, maybe," Heath said, but he doubted it. "Let's go." He knew that if the wall was on their left side coming here then it should be on their right side going back. He waved for Hadden to follow him. "We just have to walk along this wall for about five minutes I think." He started down the path that they had taken to the cave, but it looked very different from what he remembered. Heath frowned. "Maybe we're going in the wrong direction." It was all so very confusing and made him a bit scared.

Hadden followed right behind Heath. "Yeah, it does look different. Maybe we should turn around."

Heath was trying to figure it out. "No, I know that the wall was on our left side when we were heading toward the cave. It only makes sense that it would be on the opposite side of us on our way back."

Heath continued to walk and Hadden followed closely. Hadden made sure to step in the same exact spot Heath had just stepped. After what just happened, he wasn't taking any chances of ending up somewhere else like what happened when they were fighting over the gemstone.

Heath was too consumed in his thoughts to notice what Hadden was up to. *I wonder how far down we have to walk. Maybe we passed it.* Heath stopped dead in his tracks when he heard something in the distance. "I hear people talking and laughing over there," he said, pointing to the north. "That must be the way to the lake," he decided.

They changed direction and continued walking. Heath was very puzzled because he was usually pretty good with directions. He always helped his dad navigate their treasure hunts. He just couldn't figure out how he ended up so wrong.

"I don't know about this. Maybe we came from the other direction," Hadden commented.

The sound of voices was getting closer. Heath knew he was going in the right direction now. "Nah, I hear voices over there so it has to be this way." They made it to the end of the woods and stood there in complete and utter amazement once again. There wasn't a lake there, but something completely different than they expected to see.

In the distance, they saw an old-time carriage being pulled by a horse on a dirt road, children playing with a metal ring, and a woman pushing a weird-looking baby carriage down the street.

The boys looked at each other with their eyes nearly popping out of their heads. They looked back at the people that were there. "Look at their clothes, Hadden. That's what they wore a long time ago."

Hadden knew his brother was as scared and confused as he was when Heath called him by his given name.

Heath pointed to one of the children. "Look at that kid over there. He's got funny-looking shoes with buckles on 'em and his pants only go down to his knees." He thought *Maybe they are actors practicing for a play?* He hoped.

"Wait a minute!" Hadden declared. "It must be the reenactment of the Battle of Monmouth 'cause they all wear those funny clothes. That must be what it is I bet! It's June 25th and the Battle of Monmouth was on June 28th."

Heath considered it. He wasn't getting good vibes about this. "Yeah, but we are nowhere near Monmouth Battleground Park, and when they reenact a war they wear uniforms, not clothes like that. Plus, only the actors wear them but all of the people here are wearing them," he pointed out more confidently. "Someone has to be the audience. Plus the reenactment is always on a Saturday and Sunday, today is only Friday."

As they stood there soaking in the scene, another boy was walking through the woods. They were so enthralled that they never even heard him come up behind them.

"Holla," the boy said.

Hadden quickly turned around doing karate chops.

Heath spun around and fell backward into the bushes.

Hadden stopped his karate chops and stood there looking at this boy dressed in old-fashioned clothes. His fear turned to nervous amusement and he began to laugh so hard that it took a few minutes for him to calm down.

Heath stayed in the bushes in utter shock for a moment before getting himself up.

The boy in the weird gray britches gave them a strange look. When Hadden finished laughing he gave the same strange look back.

"My name is Johnny. What are you doing and why are your togs so strange?"

Heath and Hadden looked at each other and shrugged at the same time.

"Jinx," Hadden whispered out of habit.

"That's not a jinx. We didn't say anything," Heath whispered back.

Johnny simply stood there in amazement for a moment and then asked, "Are you putting a spell on me? I know that jinx is an evil spell."

"No! That's just something we say when two people say something at the same time." Heath explained.

Johnny didn't know what to make of the explanation and slowly nodded while looking at them sideways and asked, "Why are you dressed as such? You look as though you are fribble."

Hadden couldn't help himself, the boy in front of him with the strange clothes and strange words made him double over in laughter.

Heath hit Hadden on the arm to stop him from laughing.

Heath thought of the words Johnny had just used, *togs* and *fribble.* He noticed that the way everyone was dressed was how George Washington was dressed in a painting he saw at the Smithsonian Museum on their family vacation last year. His class also just learned about George Washington and the Revolutionary War. Heath finally found his voice. "I'm Heath and this is my little brother, Hadden. What are those people doing over there?" he asked as he pointed to the people out past the woods. "What reenactment is it? There aren't many people out there for a war or a battle."

Johnny just lowered his eyebrows in confusion and didn't know what to say.

"You know, how you're dressed." Heath waved his hand up and down Johnny's clothes, making the point. "What's your job, a water boy?" Heath asked.

The look on Johnny's face was now that of bewilderment. He had no idea what Heath was talking about. "I do not understand. And yes, I do water the animals. That is one of my chores of the day."

All three were speechless until Hadden finally broke the silence. "Heath, I don't like this. I'm scared. What the heck is going on?"

Johnny asked, "What are you scared of?"

"Everything," Hadden exclaimed.

Heath had been thinking long and hard about this entire

situation. "Well. Ummm. The only thing that I can think of is that something happened to us when we hit the cave wall. I had a strange feeling when we hit it. Maybe we wound up in another period of time, like the time period of George Washington," Heath said with fear in his voice. "But that's impossible." he said with more conviction.

Johnny cut him off and exclaimed, "Oh yes! George Washington, the Commander in Chief of the army of the United Colonies. Everyone knows General Washington!"

Heath went pale. *General Washington?* "Johnny, can you tell me what today is?"

"Of course! It's Tuesday, July 2nd, 1776!"

Heath felt like he was punched in the chest. His mind raced. *That's not possible. He has to be kidding me. There is no way that I'm standing here on July 2nd, 1776! No freaking way!* "No, really Johnny, seriously, what day is it?"

Sir Talks-A-Lot couldn't find any words to articulate what was going through his mind. Both of them were in utter shock and very, very scared.

Johnny didn't know what to think of Heath's response. He wondered why Heath would think he was not honest with him? Johnny said it again slowly, "Today is Tuesday, the second of July."

"And you think that the year is 1776?" Heath asked.

Johnny answered, "I do not know what year you wish it to be, however, it is 1776."

★ CHAPTER FOUR ★

JOHNNY WATCHED AS THEIR EXPRESSIONS WENT FROM confusion to utter fear. He couldn't understand what was happening. He wondered if these two bosslopers were spies for the British. He finally decided that they looked too frightened to be spies. He finally asked, "May I ask what is wrong? You look like you've seen a ghost."

Heath was so scared that his mind went completely blank for a moment. He then replayed the conversation they just had and he had no control over the tears that began forming.

Hadden, on the other hand, wasn't speechless for long. He still believed Johnny was pulling their leg. "Look, dude, I like a good joke too, but come on already, we're serious. What day is it?"

Johnny was beginning to get a little concerned for these two bosslopers. He never saw such a wardrobe, shoes, or heard their accent before. He was beginning to think that

they lost their minds. *They don't even know what day it is!*
"It truly is Tuesday, July 2, 1776."

Johnny appeared to be harmless and Heath didn't know what to do other than to be honest with him. He wiped his eyes with the back of his hand and said, "Johnny, I know you're not going to believe this but when I woke up this morning it was June 25th, 2024."

Johnny was not expecting something as far-fetched a story such as this. He opened his mouth to ask a question, but Heath quickly held up his hand to gesture to him not to talk just yet. "I know you won't believe me because I don't believe it myself, but it's true," he insisted. "But if it's true and it really is 1776, something terrible has happened. We were exploring a cave when I found a shiny green gemstone. I let Hadden look at it and he wouldn't give it back to me and..."

"You wouldn't say the magic word," Hadden interrupted.

Heath ignored him and continued. "So we started fighting over it and when we tumbled into the wall of the cave all of a sudden we were here."

The look of bewilderment on Johnny's face was obvious.

"I know it sounds crazy," Hadden said, holding his right hand up. "But it's true."

"Yes, it's true. I don't know how it happened or how we got here, but now I don't know what to do to get back home," Heath explained.

"Heath, what if we never get back home?" Hadden said with tears beginning to form in his eyes.

"We will. I don't know how or when, but I know we will get back home somehow," Heath said reassuringly, hoping to calm Hadden. Deep inside though, he was just as scared and wanted to cry too, but felt he had to be strong for his little brother so he held back the tears that wanted to form again.

"Let me think about this for a moment," Johnny said. He thought that these two lads were completely making up this story, or completely mad. He thought about the situation long and hard. *Could they be spies for the British? Are they just lunatics that escaped from somewhere? Why are they dressed in such strange clothes? What is on their feet and what is it made out of? Maybe they are from 2024.* Finally, his gut told him that these lads were telling the truth. After much consideration, Johnny said, "Well, whatever it is, there is no point in being in a feez about it right now. The only thing I believe we can do is talk to my mother about this. My mother is very wise and maybe she can help you. Come, we will ask my mother."

Heath and Hadden weren't sure if that was a good idea, but they didn't know what else to do so they agreed to go with Johnny. He led the way through the woods to his home with the brothers trailing behind.

Hadden was now back to his chatty ol' self. "So, how old are you, Johnny?"

"I will be ten years old in nine more days. I was born on July 11th, 1767."

Hadden enthusiastically pointed to each one of them as he said, "So right now we are both nine years old but in nine more days all three of us will be nine, ten, and eleven!"

Usually, Heath would have had something obnoxious to say about his little brother's chatter, but he was too wrapped up in his thoughts and worried about the situation they were in. When Heath was worried about something he was very quiet. Hadden on the other hand, well, nothing ever stopped him from talking. Even falling through a time portal didn't stop him for long.

"What do you think your mom is going to say?" Hadden asked Johnny.

"I do not know, but she will get down to the bottom of it all, I'm sure, and help you find your way home. Mama is very wise," he reassured him.

After a few minutes of walking through the woods, they made it to a clearing. Johnny stopped.

Heath and Hadden looked out into the field of grass that appeared not to have seen rain in some time. There were two houses in the distance with barns in the back.

"Wait here behind this tree," Johnny said. "Before we go inside I would like to see if there is anyone around that may see you."

"So what if they see us?" Hadden asked.

Scanning the area, Johnny explained, "I don't want to have to explain why your clothes are so different from the norm."

"Oh, okay, gotcha," Hadden said as he squatted down and leaned against the tree. Heath sat down across from him, still deep in thought.

Before Johnny walked away, Heath blurted out another question. "Is this Freehold, New Jersey?" he asked, hoping they were at least near home.

Johnny looked shocked. "No. We are in Braintree, Massachusetts." When he realized they were from New Jersey he said with excitement, "You are from one of the colonies too!"

If Heath had any color left in him, he would have lost it with that information. He grew more worried about the situation they were in.

"Alright, wait here for a moment," Johnny said. "When it is safe from onlookers I will wave to you, then you both come running over to that second house over there." He pointed to his house in the distance.

Both brothers nodded in understanding.

Johnny turned around and looked both ways before leaving the woods and running home.

Heath glared at Hadden. "You know, we wouldn't be here if you just gave me the gemstone," he said bitterly. "Wait, where is it? I wanted to give it to Mom."

Hadden looked at Heath with surprise. "What makes you think that I don't have it and what's Mom gonna do with it?"

"I dunno, but she can figure it out. If you don't have it, we'll have to go find it. I have a feeling that it's important."

"Nah, it's not gone," Hadden said as he pulled the gemstone out of his shorts pocket. "I put it in my pocket when we stood up after falling into 1776. I guess that's kinda what happened. Right?"

Heath was relieved that Hadden had the stone and his anxiety calmed down a bit. He shrugged and nodded in response to Hadden's question. A moment later he said, "Ya know what? I'm thinking that stone might be the reason we came here."

Hadden smirked as he slapped the sides of his knees. "You gotta be kidding me. How's that going to bring us here?"

Heath explained, "I read a story where there was a stone called a talisman. The talisman was magical and took people to different places and different times. Maybe it's the same thing. Maybe that stone is magical and it opened a doorway into the past. It did glow while you were holding it after all."

Hadden pondered this. "You mean it really did glow?"

"Yes, it glowed. That's why I think it's important, don't you?"

"Hmm. I was gonna say yeah right, but–" He shrugged and threw his hands up in wonder. "Here we are. Maybe you're right. Or maybe it's the cave itself?" Hadden questioned.

Heath still believed that it was the gemstone somehow. "Here, give it to me so you don't lose it."

Hadden looked at Heath with a side-eye. "Why do you think I'm gonna lose it?" he asked as he stuffed the gemstone back in his pocket. "I'll keep it right here where it's been this whole time. These shorts have very deep pockets and I can carry a lot of stuff in here. See, I have two Pokemon, Riolu and Squirtle, two Match Box cars, three pieces of candy and a handful of Double Bubble bubble gum, and my gum and candy wrappers from the ones that I ate already."

Heath sighed and decided to let it go. He just didn't have the energy to argue about it. "Okay, but pa-leeeeese don't lose it," he said emphatically.

"I won't."

Johnny walked along the side of his grandmother's house, then behind his house, and peeked around the corner. No servants or family members were in sight. He turned around to wave to Heath and Hadden. After a minute, they still weren't coming out of the woods, so he began to wave more aggressively to get their attention.

Finally, Hadden noticed the signal. "Hey look. There's Johnny. Let's go."

Johnny's house was one of two identical houses that sat on the land. Johnny and his parents and three siblings lived in one house and his grandmother lived in the other. The houses weren't massive like the McMansions they built in the year 2024. They were much smaller saltbox style homes with one story in the back and two stories in the front. The saltbox houses were known for the slanted roof in the back going from the second story down to the first. The front of the house featured five simple windows: three evenly spaced on the second story and two windows on the first story, one on either side of the front door. There was no porch, just one concrete step into the home.

"What took you so long?" Johnny asked when the boys reached him. "I was out here waving my arms like a raving madman."

They both shrugged and didn't answer.

Johnny shook his head and smirked, thinking they were probably bickering as brothers do. He gestured for them to follow him. "Come." They walked around to the side door of the house.

The boys walked into a room that appeared to be a study. As they entered, a big light brown dog came running up to greet them. The dog's tongue was flapping and his ears bobbed up and down with each step as he ran towards them.

Johnny yelled, "Satan, no!"

Hadden froze in place as he watched this giant dog come bounding towards him, and when he heard its name he went pale.

"Satan, sit," Johnny commanded. The dog obeyed and came sliding into a seated position in front of Heath and Hadden, his tail was wagging so fast that his body wiggled.

"This is Satan," Johnny said. "He's a mutt, but he's the best mutt anyone could ever have."

If Heath's eyebrows could have gone any further up they would have become bangs. "His name is Satan!?" He exclaimed.

"Oh yes, Satan is Papa's dog and he named him. I think he likes the shock that he gets when people hear the name," Johnny said with a laugh.

"Well, it definitely shocked me!" Heath admitted.

Hadden's color came back and he took a deep breath. "Whoa. I thought I was a goner there."

Johnny laughed, knowing Satan was harmless.

"Wow, he really listens to you!" Hadden said, complimenting the dog's response time. "Just like our dog, Zeus." Hadden turned to Heath. "Do you think Zeus is okay?" he asked his brother.

Heath just nodded to reassure Hadden as he looked around the room. Heath was scared to death about going through time to start with, but what were the odds that the first animal he encounterd there was named Satan? Heath wasn't liking the odds of things so far.

As Johnny continued walking into the next room, Heath noticed there weren't any lamps or lights and realized the light bulb hadn't been invented yet. The furniture in the room was spare and simple. There was a small wooden writing desk pushed up against the wall near a fireplace in the corner. Heath also noticed the tall wooden bookshelf on the opposite side of the room. He couldn't help but wonder what kinds of stories filled the books in 1776.

The next room had another bookshelf and another fireplace. Under the back window was a small wooden table with two spindly wooden chairs. Heath thought that the chairs didn't look very comfortable.

They continued through into a third room with an even bigger fireplace, so long that it almost took up the whole wall. Next to the fireplace, there was a small square opening built into the wall that appeared to be a brick oven. Although there wasn't a refrigerator, a stove, or a sink, Heath and Hadden could tell immediately that this was the kitchen. A black pot hung from a metal rack and swung in and out of the fireplace. Heath thought it looked like a witch's cauldron that she'd make potions in. Mason jars filled with fruits and vegetables, plates, cups, and ceramic jars lined the shelves on the wall near the back door. A woman and a girl were standing at the table, where it looked like they were beating up dough.

"Mama, this is Heath and Hadden whom I met on my walk through the woods," Johnny said as they entered. "They say that they are not from around here and are lost. Maybe you might be able to help them get back home."

Johnny's mother was a pretty woman with dark brown hair and brown eyes. She turned to the boys with flour all over her hands as she wiped them on the front of her dress. Hadden suspected that she was making a cake because Mom always had flour all over her hands when she baked cakes. Mom just didn't wipe it all over her clothes. After his thought, he realized that she was wearing an apron.

"Ah, so you two are what is making Satan so excited," Johnny's mother said with a warm and inviting smile.

"Heath, Hadden, this is my mother, Mrs. Adams," Johnny said. He nodded at the girl at the table. "That's my sister Nabby."

Nabby was ten years old and was helping her mother bake bread. She had long red hair, a round face, deep blue eyes, and was very shy. She wore a dress and an apron just like her mother and they both wore caps on their heads.

"Hello, Mrs. Adams," Heath said as he stepped towards the woman. He nudged Hadden's side with his elbow as a cue to be polite and greet her as well.

Hadden gave Heath the stink eye, then nudged him back. He turned his head towards the ladies and said, "Hello Mrs. Adams," and to one-up his brother he said, "and hello Nabby." He then turned back to Heath and stuck out his tongue feeling like he made the better impression.

"I want to apologize if Satan scared you," said Mrs. Adams. "He gets so excited when we have new guests."

Hadden squatted to pet Satan. "That's okay, Satan is a great dog! We have a dog too. His name is Zeus."

Mrs. Adams placed the bread she and Nabby were working on in the brick oven. "That's a wonderful name. Does he behave, or does he go running up and scare strangers at your door also?" she asked as she took off her cap and apron.

"Yeah, he barks and sounds really mean to people until they come in. Then he tries to hug them like he's their best friend or something. He's really smart. He knows all sorts of tricks, but we can't get him to stop barking until we open the door and allow him to greet whoever is there," Hadden said, shaking his head.

Hadden's description of Zeus reminded Johnny of the story of Mama and General Charles Lee's dog, a Pomeranian. "Mama went to a dinner party with the generals of the Continental Army a few months back," he laughed. "General Lee brought his dog, Spada, with him. He placed a chair in front of Mama and commanded Spada to sit on the chair and shake hands. Mama had no choice but to shake the dog's paw!" When Johnny finished telling the story everyone laughed except for Heath and Mrs. Adams.

Heath wasn't really paying any attention to the conversation. His mind was wandering. He was bewildered over the fact that he went from his little hometown of Freehold, New Jersey, to Massachusetts. Then it dawned on him that not only could the gemstone, cave, or whatever take you to a different date and time, but it could also take you to any place it wanted to from the cave at Culver's Cove.

Mrs. Adams was also distracted. Her thoughts were on the boys' clothes and the way they spoke. She noticed they said hello and not holla as a greeting. She wondered where the boys were from. Mrs. Adams knew that a lot of people were coming to the colonies from all over the world and she wondered if they were foreign. "So what country are you from?" she asked.

Heath realized that she was probably thinking that they were from China or something. He didn't know how to tell her that he was from the future. While he was still deciding what to say his mouth suddenly had a brain of its own and he blurted out, "We're from Timbuktu."

Hadden's head swung around so fast that you could almost hear the swoosh it made as he turned it to look at Heath with utter surprise.

Heath wasn't fast enough with his elbow to Hadden's arm to try to stop him from saying anything.

"Whaaat?" Hadden rolled his eyes, thinking that Heath must be losing his marbles in all this chaos. "No we're not," he said. "We're from the United States of America."

Heath was mortified. *There isn't a United States just yet.* He didn't know how to fix this situation that Hadden created by opening his big mouth. All Heath could do was just stand there waiting for Mrs. Adams to say something.

"Timbuktu, you say?" Mrs. Adams questioned. She went over to the table, pulled out a chair, and took a seat.

As Mrs. Adams continued to ponder things, the front door opened and the sound of little bare feet came running into the kitchen. Two little boys with dark brown hair and brown eyes entered. The first little boy had a scrape on his knee. The second one was smaller than the first and was holding the hand of another woman.

"Mary," Mrs. Adams said. "This is Hadden and Heath," she said as she nodded in the boys' direction.

The child let go of the woman's hand and went running over to Mrs. Adams. She picked him up and placed him on her lap. "Boys, these are my other sons. This little lad right here is Tommy. He's four, and over there is Charlie. He's six. Mary is one of our servants," she explained.

Mary was a tiny lady with black hair and brown eyes, about thirty years old. She was in a dress and apron just like Mrs. Adams. "It's very nice to meet you," she said to the boys. She turned to Mrs. Adams and said, "Ma'am, I'm going to get started on churning the butter now. Unless there is something else that needs to be done first."

"No, that's fine, Mary. Thank you."

Mary nodded and walked out the back door from the kitchen.

Mrs. Adams turned to look at her daughter. "Nabby, would you take Charlie and Tommy outside and entertain them for a bit? I'd like to talk with Heath and Hadden for a moment."

Heath and Hadden looked at each other with wide eyes and took a big gulp.

Nabby nodded and reached for the child on her mother's lap. "Come 'ere, Tommy." He willingly reached up for Nabby to pick him up and place him on the floor. Then she extended her hand to Charlie to take his hand but he resisted.

"I don't want to go outside, it's hot out there," Charlie whined.

Nabby seemed to know just how to handle her little brothers. She knelt down to eye level with Charlie and said, "Mama needs us to go and pick some flowers for the table," she said in a sweet and patient tone. "I can't do it myself. Would you help me?"

Charlie looked around. With nothing that seemed interesting enough to stay inside, he started for the back door. "I'll pick the white ones with the yellow middles."

Nabby chased him out the door. "Yes, but wait for me, Charlie."

Mrs. Adams pointed to empty chairs at the table. "Please have a seat, boys."

Johnny pulled a chair out and sat down. Heath and Hadden both tried to take the same chair that was closest to them. Heath came around the right side of it to sit as Hadden tried to sit on it from the left. Both half on the chair, they both thought it was rightfully theirs and they pushed themselves further onto the seat trying to knock the other off. Hadden turned halfway around to look Heath in the eye to say something and lifted one buttcheek off the chair. Heath seized the opportunity and pushed Hadden off completely. Hadden slid off but landed on his feet. He lightly backhanded Heath in the arm, admitting defeat, and began walking around the table to the chair across from Heath. He was too busy giving Heath the stink eye as he walked around the table and he tripped over his own foot. THUMP!

Mrs. Adams looked at Hadden and calmly asked, "Are you alright there, dear?"

"Yeah, sometimes my feet just get in my way."

Heath rolled his eyes and shook his head.

Mrs. Adams and Johnny smiled.

Heath realized that Mrs. Adams didn't get all worried like Mrs. Peterson, Danny's mom from next door. Any time a kid fell Mrs. Peterson always went running over to them all hysterically. Once he fell off his skateboard in front of their house and Mrs. Peterson ran over yelling, "Oh my gosh! Are you alright? Oh no, what did you do to yourself? Let me see. Do you need me to get your mother? I hope nothing is broken." Luckily Mom heard her and came out to save him from Mrs. Peterson's "love". Well, that's what Mom told him it was when he said she was crazy. Mom said, "Don't say that. She just loves all you kids and is concerned about you." He decided that he liked Johnny's mom. Then he got really scared that he wouldn't see his mom ever again. *I want my mom! I hope Mrs. Adams knows how to help us*, he thought as he sat there patiently waiting, holding back tears.

Johnny decided to begin the conversation. "Ma, Heath and Hadden..." He paused. He didn't know how to begin.

Mrs. Adams pressed on, "Heath and Hadden what, dear?"

Heath remembered watching a cartoon and even a movie where a kid ended up back in time. The kid never told anyone and became a hero all on his own with no help from any adults whatsoever. He knew he wasn't on a TV show or in a movie and he certainly didn't feel like a hero. He was scared and so confused as to what to do. He then remembered Mom always said to tell the truth no matter what. She always said lies always have a way of getting you deeper and deeper into trouble. Being in the year 1776 was the scariest thing that Heath had ever experienced. Even his nightmares weren't this scary. He was getting pretty close to crying. He spoke up before Johnny could reply. "Me and Hadden, I mean, Hadden and I are from a very, very far away place."

"It's so far away it's gonna blow your mind," Hadden added as he waved his hand for emphasis.

Mrs. Adams and Johnny had a look of confusion at Hadden's statement.

Heath tried kicking him under the table. He missed because Hadden liked to swing his feet back and forth while sitting at the table. He tried again and kicked Hadden's leg.

"Owww! Why did you kick me, ya little corn muffin?"

Heath ignored him and looked over at Mrs. Adams who had one eyebrow raised and the other lowered. "We were exploring a cave and I found a cool-looking gemstone. It seemed like it was shining just to get my attention or something. It was really weird. And then Hadden wanted to see it so I gave it to him to look at for a second and when I wanted it back he wouldn't let me have it."

"You wouldn't say the magic word."

Heath didn't acknowledge Hadden's comment. He held his head down looking at his fingers as he twiddled his thumbs as he continued the story. "We started fighting over it. We wrestled and tumbled into the wall of the cave and all of a sudden we were here." Heath lifted his head to look at Mrs. Adams. "Johnny found us and told us that the year was 1776, but Mrs. Adams, we were just in the year 2024."

★ CHAPTER FIVE ★

HEATH, HADDEN, AND JOHNNY SAT AT THE TABLE ANX-iously waiting to see what Mrs. Adams' reaction was going to be. She seemed pretty shocked at their story and didn't immediately comment. All three boys were on the edge of their seats in anticipation of her response. Mrs. Adams remembered that she had once heard of a story about someone claiming that they were from another time period after going into a cave, but she shrugged it off as nonsense. Now, these two lads with their strange names, odd clothes, and accents were sitting in her kitchen with the same story. She wondered why two little boys would make up such nonsense. What would be the point she wondered? She looked up from the table and asked, "What state are you from?" directing her question to Hadden.

"New Jersey," he quickly answered before Heath got all weird on him again.

Mrs. Adams gave a slow nod as she looked out the window. "And you say you just wound up here in Massachusetts from New Jersey." She looked back at Heath. "In the year 1776 from the year 2024?"

Heath and Hadden nodded in unison. They were both petrified of what was to come next.

Johnny just sat there, with his arms folded on the table, patiently watching his mother's reaction unfold.

Mrs. Adams was a very articulate woman. She was intelligent, independent, open-minded, and confident. Her husband, John, was away from home for work much of the time so she handled all family affairs by herself. She was responsible for attending to the farm, managing the finances, maintaining the home, teaching the children, and overseeing the servants. She seemed to juggle it all with ease and even found time to lend a helping hand to anyone who needed it. She believed in civil rights and the rights of women. Her beliefs were very strongly held and given the opportunity she would have fought to the death to defend them. Although, right at this moment in time, she wasn't too sure what she believed. She wished her husband were here to get his opinion on this troublesome affair. She slowly stood up from her chair.

Hadden sat there swinging his feet back and forth and wondered what Mrs. Adams could be thinking. He thought maybe she was mad and was going to kick them out. He just couldn't handle the quiet any longer and asked, "So, do you know what we have to do to get home, Mrs. Adams?"

"Well, this story is a pretty big one," she finally said.

"It's not a story, it's the whole truth. I promise," Hadden said as he held up his right hand.

Johnny finally piped up. "Ma, I know it sounds preposterous but look at their clothes. Listen to their accents. I believe them!"

Neither Heath nor Hadden knew what preposterous meant, but Hadden thought that since Johnny seemed to believe them hopefully it meant something good.

Mrs. Adams rubbed both sides of her head on her temples with her fingers. "I must take a moment to think about this. Johnny, take the boys upstairs and look through your old clothes to find something for them to wear, please."

Heath knew what Mrs. Adams was trying to do. She wanted the boys to look like they fit in this time period. With their T-shirts, shorts, and sneakers they would stand out like a Froot Loop in a bowl of Cheerios.

"Yes ma'am." Johnny slid off his chair and headed towards the door of the kitchen. "Come on," he said to the boys.

Heath and Hadden got up and followed Johnny into the next room.

Johnny led them out of the kitchen through a narrow hallway. They passed a door on the right, which Heath assumed was the door to the basement. At the end of the little hallway, they entered the room known as the parlor. This was where Mrs. Adams had visitors, made quilts and clothes, and did her knitting. It's also where she read and wrote letters. There was a fancy red couch near the fireplace and a colorful rug with red and blue flowers on it.

"Wow. You have a fireplace in every room!" Hadden marveled.

The room also had a spinning wheel in front of the window. It was a wooden wheel attached to a flat piece of wood that sat on three legs and had a pedal underneath it. There was a chair near the wheel and a basket on the floor next to it filled with yarn.

Heath noticed that there were lots of candles in the room. Metal candle stands stood in two corners of the room, about three feet tall, and held three candles each. On the fireplace mantle, there were two small candles in round candle holders that had little loops on the bottom where a finger was used to hold them. Heath turned to his left and saw a similar candle holder on the desk, along with parchment to write on with a small black ink jar and a bird's feather. Heath knew the feather was for writing because the ballpoint pen hadn't been invented yet.

Hadden, on the other hand, got wide-eyed with excitement when he saw the feather. "Whoa! Look at the size of this feather!" he yelled as he went to get a closer look.

Johnny found this funny. He never saw anyone get so excited over a quill before.

"That is Mama's desk. That's where she writes letters to Papa as often as she can."

"Where's your dad that your mom has to write to him?" Heath asked.

"Oh, he has been in Pennsylvania for work for a while now," he replied as he continued through the room to the front foyer of the house. Johnny turned right and headed up the weird stairs with Hadden trailing right behind him. Heath looked ahead to the room on the opposite side of the foyer; it looked familiar. He stuck his head through the door-frame to check it out and realized it was the study where they had entered the house. They had just walked around the first floor in a big circle.

Suddenly, Heath heard a bang and then a "Yee ouch!" He knew Hadden had fallen and quickly turned around to head upstairs. He got one foot on the bottom step before Satan ran past. Satan ran up the steps to where Hadden was sitting holding his knee and licked the side of his face with his big wet tongue and continued up the stairs and into the room on the left.

Heath hurried to the stairs, which reminded him of Mom's paper fold-up fan. They curved to the left behind a wall, making the stairs turn a quick left, which created narrow steps. *No wonder he tripped, it's not easy going up these steps.* He looked up at Hadden from a few steps below. "These are some pretty weird steps."

Hadden was getting up from the step and shrugged off

the incident. "Yeah, I never saw any like this before and I hope I never do again."

"Yeah, me either. Just be careful so you don't go breakin' something."

Johnny was at the top of the stairs. "I fell a couple of times myself. You do get used to them." He then turned around and disappeared into the same room Satan ran into.

When they finally made it to the top, Hadden followed Johnny into the bedroom but Heath stopped before the bedroom to look out of the window. The window overlooked the front yard and Heath could see for miles. He saw a dirt road, fields of crops, barns to the left and to the right, animals roaming around in their paddocks, and a clothesline with freshly washed clothes hanging to dry.

Heath heard a noise coming from the bedroom where Hadden and Johnny were. He walked in and found Johnny rummaging through a big chest of clothes on the floor. Satan was on the bed watching from above.

"These are my knickerbockers from last year. I think they will fit you," he said, handing them to Heath. Johnny turned around and picked up another pair of knickerbockers and handed them to Hadden. "Here, I believe this might be a bit small but it should be alright." He picked through the chest again and found two shirts. "And here, give this a go," he said as he tossed them to the boys. He looked down at their strange shoes and scratched his head. "I don't know what to do about your feet. I only have one pair of shoes and I am currently wearing them."

Heath couldn't believe that Johnny only had one pair of shoes. They each had several pairs at home. They had school shoes, dress shoes, play shoes, boots, sneakers, and even summer shoes.

"Well, would it look funny if we just took our shoes off and walked around barefoot?" Heath asked.

"Hmm, maybe that's the only thing we can do. Well, a lot of kids don't bother wearing shoes in the summer so that won't be so different. I prefer to wear shoes because I stepped on a bee three years in a row. I will leave now so you two can change your clothes. Just come down when you are finished." Johnny left the room and Satan jumped off the bed to follow him downstairs. Heath stood there a moment looking around the room. The bed had a canopy with curtains tied on every corner. He figured this must be Nabby's room because of the curtains on the bed, but he couldn't understand why the chest of boys' clothes would be in a girl's room. There were even boys' toys such as a wooden horse on the floor in the corner.

Heath slipped off his shorts and pulled on the knickers. They were brown pants that stopped just past the knee. They had built-in suspenders that functioned with buttons in the front. Heath shook his head and noted that they didn't have zippers back then. The shirt was a long sleeve white shirt with ruffles at the wrists.

Hadden leaned against the bed and took off his shorts. As he lifted his right foot to put it into the leg of the knickers he stumbled forward and fell. CAPLUNK.

Heath shook his head and smiled, "You goofball."

For the past five minutes, Hadden had been reflecting on all that has happened. He was petrified that he would never see his mom and dad again. He wondered what would happen if they never found a way home and had to stay here forever. He had a lot on his mind for a little kid of nine. Hadden looked up and glared at Heath then continued to put on the knickers while sitting on the floor.

That's when Heath realized that Hadden had been pretty quiet for a bit. "Hey, we will get back home," he said as he tucked the shirt into the knickers. "We got here somehow so there is a way to get back home. I just know it. So don't worry. Okay?"

Hadden just nodded his head and stood up. He picked up the shirt that was on the bed to put it on.

"Hey, if I had to come here," Heath said, "I'm glad that you're here with me too." He laid his hand on Hadden's shoulder and smiled, hoping to cheer him up a little. Hadden's silence was secretly killing him.

Hadden gave him a slight grin.

"Ready?"

Hadden nodded.

In the kitchen, Mrs. Adams and Johnny were sitting at the table. Satan was lying in the corner beside Johnny. It wasn't hard to see whom Satan liked around here.

Mrs. Adams looked their clothes up and down. "Well, I suppose it will do."

Shifting uncomfortably, Heath sat at the table where he was seated earlier.

Hadden looked at Mrs. Adams and asked, "Can I use your bathroom?"

Mrs. Adams tilted her head trying to understand. She then looked over at Johnny for help.

He replied with a shoulder shrug and a shake of his head.

Mrs. Adams then turned back to Hadden and said, "Pardon me?"

This reminded Hadden of when his mom would sometimes correct him when he didn't ask for something properly. "Oh, sorry. *May* I *please* use your bathroom?"

"I do apologize," Mrs. Adams said with an apologetic smile. "But I don't know what you are asking me."

Heath realized they didn't have bathrooms yet. To demonstrate what his brother needed, he stood up, placed his hands in front of his crotch, jumped around a bit, and yelled, "Ooooh. Ooooh. Ooooh. I gotta go!"

Mrs. Adams and Johnny's faces lit up with acknowledgment.

"Oh, yes! Johnny, please show Hadden where the privy is."

Heath and Hadden looked at each other and smirked. They both knew that the other one was thinking the same thing. *Privy. What a funny word.*

"Why don't you go with them, Heath, so you know where it is also," Mrs. Adams suggested.

Johnny jumped off his seat and headed to the back door with Satan close behind him.

Hadden started to follow him and noticed he was headed outside. "Wait, where are you going? I have to use the bathroom."

Johnny paused, looking puzzled.

Heath came up from behind him and put his arm around Hadden's shoulder encouraging him to continue to walk forward and whispered, "They don't have bathrooms here. They have little shacks outside that they use to go to the bathroom in. I think they are called outhouses."

Johnny overheard Heath. "We don't call it a shack or an outhouse. We call it the necessary or the privy."

Hadden began jumping around a bit and said, "Okay, the privy is necessary right now. Can we go?"

Johnny laughed as he opened the door and Satan went running out first. Johnny led them through the backyard, around the barn, and pointed to a small, skinny shack with a roof. It kind of resembled a doghouse except it was a lot taller and had a door. "There is the privy," Johnny said as he pointed to it.

Hadden opened the door and was taken aback by the smell. "Oh, my God!" It smelled like something died with a hint of stinky feet, mixed with poo, then mixed with rotten food. Instead of the toilet that he was used to, there was just a piece of wood that ran the width of the shack with a hole in the center of it. Against the wall was a small bucket filled with water and corn cobs. Hadden stood there a moment, holding the door open, allowing his brain to process the scene. He turned around to look at Heath and whispered, "Are you kidding me?"

"No. That is where you go, ya dork," Heath said with a smirk.

Hadden went in and closed the door behind him. Having Heath call him a dork, after all this time, felt good and he was able to relax a little more since Heath seemed a little more at ease.

Johnny heard Hadden's question and asked, "May I ask you a question?"

Heath shrugged. "Sure."

Johnny leaned up on a nearby fence and placed his foot on the bottom rail. "Where do you keep your privy? Hadden had no idea that the privy was outside."

"Our bathrooms are in our houses."

Johnny was aghast. "Why would you have the privy in your house? The stench alone must be unimaginably bad."

Hadden could hear Johnny's questions from inside the privy and began to laugh. It felt good to laugh. After being tossed into 1776 and being scared of never returning home, laughing felt normal. Hadden was able to lighten up a lot more, especially now that he was relieved.

Heath began to try and explain what bathrooms were. "In our time we have rooms in the house that have a toilet where you do your business. When you are done you push a button and it just goes down the toilet."

Johnny was really trying hard to understand. It was baffling to him. "What is a toilet?"

Heath looked off into the distance trying to figure out how to explain what it is. "Well, um..."

Hadden swung open the privy door laughing. "Sometimes we call it the royal throne."

Heath rolled his eyes and shook his head knowing that didn't help.

"Hey, Johnny," Hadden yelled as he walked towards the two of them. "What do you do if you have to go number two?"

Johnny chuckled. "Number two?"

"Yeah. What do you use to wipe your butt?" Hadden asked as he wiped at his backside with his hand for effect.

Johnny laughed. "We use newspapers or corn cobs that are in the privy."

"That's why there are corn cobs in there? Boy, I hope I don't have to go poo anytime soon," Hadden said while he scrunched up his nose. His reaction made Johnny laugh even more.

Looking at the outhouse reminded Heath of a joke. "Johnny, do you wanna hear a joke?"

"Oh yes, indeed!"

"Once there was a little boy who lived in the country. They had to use an outhouse, or a privy, and the little boy hated it because it was hot in the summer, cold in the winter and stank ALL the time. The privy was sitting on the bank of a creek and the boy said that one day he would push that privy into the creek. One day after a spring rain, the creek got so big that the little boy decided today was the day to push the privy into the creek. So he got a large stick and started pushing. Finally, the privy toppled into the creek and floated away. That night his dad told him they were going to the woodshed after supper. Knowing that meant a spanking, the little boy asked why. The dad replied, 'Someone pushed the privy into the creek today. It was you, wasn't it, son?' The boy couldn't tell a lie and answered yes. Then he thought for a moment and said, 'Dad, I heard that George Washington chopped down a cherry tree and didn't get into trouble because he told the truth,' and the dad said, 'Well, son, George Washington's father wasn't in that cherry tree.'

Johnny laughed so hard that he held his stomach as

he laughed. Heath enjoyed making people laugh and he smiled watching Johnny.

When Johnny stopped laughing he said, "That was a great joke. I am guessing that jokes are stories that make people laugh."

"There are long ones and there are short ones. That was a long one, here's a short one, why are there no knock-knock jokes about America?" Heath asked.

Johnny furrowed his eyebrows wondering what the answer could possibly be. "I don't know why there are no knock knock jokes about America. Do tell me."

Heath smiled at Johnny's answer and answered his question. "There are no knock knock jokes about America because freedom rings."

Johnny didn't understand the joke but didn't want to be rude so he just smiled. Satan came running up with a stick and Johnny picked it up and threw it for him. With the stick in his mouth, Satan ran ahead of them towards the house.

When they entered the house all three boys made their way to their seats at the table. Satan laid down in his usual corner next to Johnny. He panted, as it was too hot for any man or beast to exert themselves too much.

"Ma, I believed their story before, but now I *know* they are from the future," Johnny said, pulling a chair out to sit down. "They say they have a room with a privy *in the house*. They call it a bathroom!" He looked at Heath. "Correct?"

Heath and Hadden nodded in unison and Hadden said, "Yeah, and there's a sink and a bathtub in there too."

Mrs. Adams looked interested. She didn't speak for a moment. Then she said, "Well, that is something that I would really like to hear more about, but I think we have more important things to discuss right now." She turned her body to face the boys as she folded her hands. "I have been thinking a lot about your story."

"It's not a story, Mrs. Adams," Hadden insisted. "It's what really and truly happened to us. I promise. My mom always says that when you say I promise, you better make sure you keep your promise because it shows what kind of a person you are." Hadden looked at Heath for confirmation. "If you don't keep your promises then you can't be trusted, right?"

Heath nodded.

Hadden looked back at Mrs. Adams and raised his hand up as he said, "You can trust us, Mrs. Adams, I promise!"

Mrs. Adams smiled. "You two have a very clear mother and I'm sure that you both are honorable young men."

Mrs. Adams was quiet as she gathered her thoughts. She was vulnerable to migraines and thought one was going to begin shortly. She rubbed her forehead as she looked down at her lap. She looked up at the boys and took a deep breath. "Boys, I consider myself to have an open mind and can imagine things that may happen in the future. For example, it is my hope that one day we will be free from British rule."

"What?" Hadden wondered.

Mrs. Adams looked at Hadden. "Go ahead. Finish your sentence."

"I did. I said what, like, what are you talking about?"

Mrs. Adams nodded her head in acknowledgment. "Oh. Well, right now, America is run by King George III, and he is making us pay taxes that we rightfully should not have to pay without someone there speaking up for us in their government. First, it was the Stamp Act, then the Townshend Acts, and then it was the tax on tea."

Heath got excited. "I know about that!" he shouted. "The Boston Tea Party! The people dressed like Indians and jumped onto the ship that was bringing the tea and smashed all the tea and then knocked it over into the water!"

Mrs. Adams was impressed. "Yes! You are correct! Very good, young man!"

Heath beamed with pride.

"Well, if you really are from the year 2024, then I am guessing that you would know all about that and beyond," Mrs. Adams said. "What do you know about it?"

"Well, after the Boston Tea Party, King George, and the British Parliament passed the Coercive Acts or the Intolerable Acts. These acts closed Boston Harbor until the tea that was lost was paid for and a few other things. Britain hoped that it would help stop the rebellion in New England and stop the other colonies from uniting. But it had the opposite effect. The colonies looked at it as Britain still trying to tell them what to do."

"Yes, it is a bit more than that though, I'm afraid. King George has been a tyrant for a very long time. He has done a lot more than just tax us. There are over twenty things that I can list off the top of my head where he was just atrocious. However, we are getting off the subject which I wanted to discuss. I mentioned that I could imagine our separation from England. I can even imagine that one day women will have equal rights as men and slavery will be a horrible memory. However." She paused for a second and her eyes went to Heath and then to Hadden. "I find it extremely hard to imagine time travel."

Hadden opened his mouth, ready to say something, but Mrs. Adams held her hand up in the universal gesture to stop him from talking. "Wait. Let me finish, please." She put her hand down. "But even though I do find it difficult to imagine such a thing, I am open-minded enough to believe that it could be true."

★ CHAPTER SIX ★

HEATH AND HADDEN WERE HAPPY TO HEAR THAT MRS. Adams "kinda" believed them. She didn't think that they were crazy at least. Nabby came through the back door carrying Tommy, who was crying. Charlie came following in behind her carrying freshly picked daisies. "Tommy fell and hit his knee on a stone. He's not hurt, but I do believe that he is very tired," Nabby explained as she placed the boy on a chair.

Tommy looked up at Hadden with tears in his eyes, which made Hadden and Heath feel that they should be doing something to help, but just didn't know what to do. They felt bad for the little guy when he sniffled and wiped his nose on the back of his hand.

Hearing the child's cry, Satan jumped to the rescue once again. He quickly went over to Tommy to assess the situation. He sniffed the boy, licked his leg, and determined that it wasn't too bad so he decided to head out back. Satan made his exit as Mrs. Adams said, "I do think it is time for dinner and a nap for these two."

Heath and Hadden raised their eyebrows in disbelief. "Dinner? In the middle of the afternoon?" Hadden questioned.

"Well, don't you have to nourish yourself in the mid-afternoon?" Nabby asked with surprise.

"Yeah, but we call it lunch."

Mrs. Adams picked Tommy up to comfort him. "Well, whatever you would like to call it. Let's first feed Tommy and Charlie so Tommy can have his afternoon nap." She said to Johnny, "Why don't you entertain the boys while Nabby and I get something for din, uh, lunch and put Tommy down." She looked at Hadden and smiled.

Hadden couldn't help but smile back.

The boys jumped off their chairs and walked out the back door with Johnny as he was saying, "I will show them around the farm."

Outside, the boys noticed Mary sitting in the shade of a tall oak tree. It was getting hot and even Satan was in a hole in the shade of the tree. Mary sat atop a tall round wooden barrel with a wooden stick that she was moving up and down. Hadden pointed to her and asked, "What is she doing?"

Johnny glanced over toward Mary. "Oh, she's churning butter. I am guessing that you have never seen that before?"

Hadden shook his head. "No."

Johnny walked Heath and Hadden over to where Mary sat churning butter and asked, "Ms. Mary, would you show us how this works in order to make butter? I never thought of it myself until Hadden asked about it. Now I am curious too."

Mary looked up and smiled. "Of course."

Satan lifted his head as if acknowledging Johnny was there but then put it back down, deciding that it was too hot to move.

While Mary was pulling the stick up and pushing it back down, she began to explain, "When we milk the cows..."

Hadden interrupted with, "You milk cows! Can I milk a cow?"

Mary and Johnny laughed and Mary said, "Of course! I'll be happy to show you, but first, let's finish with the butter. When we milk the cows, we take the milk and place it in shallow dishes and store them in a cool place. We wait about half a day or so and let the cream rise to the top. Then we take a skimmer and scoop off the cream from the top of the milk. Then we place the cream in this churn and keep mixing it up to take away all the fat from the cream. After a while, it splits and I scoop out the butter. What is left is called buttermilk."

Heath and Hadden were impressed. They only knew of going to the store and buying butter already made. Hadden said, "Wow, they make *everything* here, even butter!"

"Johnny, why don't you take them over to see the cows while I keep churning a bit more and then come back and we can milk the cows?" Mary suggested.

Hadden's eyes lit up as he said, "Yeah, let's go see the cows!"

"Alright, follow me." With Johnny and the boys walking away, Satan wasn't going to miss something and took off after them.

Johnny took them to a fenced-in field where the cows were roaming around freely. The fence was a simple one. It had vertical line posts with just two horizontal planks. Johnny climbed up on the bottom plank and threw his arms over the top. Heath and Hadden did the same, one on either side of Johnny, and they all looked over at the cows.

Satan wandered along the fence until he came to a tree and laid down in the shade. Johnny pointed out to the field and said, "The one farthest away is my favorite. I call her Clara."

Hadden pointed to a cow that was over to his right and said, "I think I like him the best."

Johnny began to laugh. Heath and Hadden had no idea what was so funny.

"The cows are all girls," Johnny said. "That's why we can milk them. The males are in another field. They are used for mating and meat while the females are for babies and milk."

Heath saw another barn beside the cow barn. Actually, there were a few barns here. He knew that if it had a fence in front of it, it was probably for animals that were in the barn. Heath pointed to a big barn that didn't have a fence in front of it. "What's in that barn over there?"

"That is where we keep farm equipment and the whiskey," Johnny said.

"Why do your parents keep their whiskey out here in the barn? My mom and dad keep the whiskey in the house."

Johnny doubled over in laughter. He was laughing so much that he couldn't answer Heath. Heath and Hadden leaned back on the fence and just looked at each other, shrugged, and shook their heads.

When Johnny finally stopped laughing, he wiped the tears from his face with one hand while still holding onto the fence with the other. He tried speaking. "You said—" and he began laughing all over again.

Hadden was getting a little annoyed now. "Okay, Johnny, it's not really that funny."

Finally, after what seemed like forever, Johnny stopped laughing. "I apologize for my laughter, but I do want to say thank you for the good laugh. Ever since the war started, it has been very hard to laugh about anything around here. It's been so stressful for everyone. A year ago on the 17th of June, Mama and I went over yonder—" He pointed to a distant hill about ten miles from his farm— "to Penn's Hill. We sat and watched the Battle of Bunker Hill there. I saw with my own eyes the fires and heard Britain's thunders of the guns and the cannons. I witnessed the tears of my mother and I cried with her. The next day we got word that a dear friend of my father, Joseph Warren, died on that day. He had been our family physician and surgeon and had saved my forefinger from amputation under a very bad fracture. I can still smell the fires and see the flames with the burning of Charlestown if I were to close my eyes right now."

While Johnny was telling his story, Heath was envisioning everything that happened in Johnny's story as if it were his own memories. He didn't think too much about it until Johnny stopped talking but Heath remembered walking down the hill with Mrs. Adams. Both he and Mrs. Adams were crying and she said, "Oh Johnny, we shall never forget this day as long as we live." Johnny didn't mention that part of the story so Heath didn't know why he thought of that scenario.

The three boys stayed on that fence post in silence for an entire two minutes. Finally, Heath couldn't help it anymore; so many weird things had been happening to him that he had to ask Johnny, "The day that you saw the battle, was your mom wearing a beige dress with brown shoes with buckles on the front of them? Did you and your mom walk down the hill after seeing that and she told you that both of you will never forget that day?"

Johnny slowly answered. "Yes, how do you know that?"

"I don't know. When you were talking about your memory, I saw it in my mind as if it were one of my memories, but when you stopped talking, I kept on remembering things after that. Weird things are happening to me lately and it's starting to freak me out, but I don't want to talk about that right now." Heath was sorry he mentioned anything. He didn't want to try and explain something so weird and have Hadden and Johnny think there's something wrong with him. "I think it's a good time to go to see if it's time to eat, don't you?" Heath asked as he jumped off the fence and started for the house.

Johnny was still curious about how Heath knew what had happened on that dreadful day and couldn't let it go. "Am I correct in saying that you saw my memory of walking home after witnessing the Battle of Bunker Hill?"

"I guess I am. It seemed crystal clear to me."

"Can you do it again?" Hadden wanted to know.

"I don't know. Think of something," Heath instructed.

Hadden thought of skipping stones on the lake with Heath and their dad last week. "Okay, what did I think about?" Hadden asked.

Heath said with disappointment, "I don't know. It didn't happen again."

"So what else is happening that's so weird?" Hadden asked. He was getting worried about his big brother now. This didn't sound like Heath at all.

"Nothing. Don't worry about it."

"No, what else is happening?" Hadden insisted.

"I will tell you all about it later," Heath responded.

As they walked back to the house, Heath listened to the birds singing, a horse neighing, and even heard a buzz from a bumble bee that flew by. He thought to himself, *Wow, I don't remember hearing sounds like these at home. There are no cars here, no lawnmowers going, and no leaf blowers. It's so quiet that you can probably hear a feather hit the ground.*

When they were almost to the door, Hadden took hold of Johnny's shoulder and asked, "Wait a minute. What was so funny before?"

"Well, you said that your parents keep the whiskey in the house. I don't know what you think whiskey is, but here it is our two-wheeled, one-horse carriage that we ride in. It whisks us around." Johnny smiled. "I just imagined it sitting in your house and began laughing. I guess it felt so good to laugh that I couldn't stop."

Heath and Hadden smiled.

"What is whiskey in your time?"

"It's something adults drink. It has alcohol in it," Heath explained.

Johnny opened the back door and Satan went running through first. As they entered the kitchen, Johnny asked, "Is dinner ready? I am getting a bit hungry."

Mrs. Adams had three bowls filled with beef, carrots,

corn, potatoes, and gravy with freshly baked bread ready to place on the table. Charlie's flowers were in a vase in the center of the table. "Yes, it was ready about twenty minutes ago. I didn't call you because I thought you and the boys might be occupied with something. I just happened to see you three from the window and filled the bowls."

Mrs. Adams placed a bowl in front of Heath and he said, "Thank you, Mrs. Adams."

Hadden followed suit with his, "Thank you," as she placed it in front of him.

Mrs. Adams smiled, "You both are welcome. I hope you like beef stew."

Heath nodded. "I love beef stew and Hadden will eat *anything!*"

Mrs. Adams and all three boys laughed.

Mrs. Adams placed glasses of milk on the table for all three boys and Hadden asked, "It looks like milk but it looks different than ours. Is this milk? It's white, but this isn't as white as ours."

"It's buttermilk. Mary just brought it in," Mrs. Adams said with a laugh.

It dawned on Heath what the difference was. "Our milk is regular milk and this is the buttermilk that Miss Mary was talking about before."

"Oooh, well, let me see if there is a difference in taste." Hadden took a sip and swooshed it around in his mouth a bit.

He looked up at the ceiling to really give it a good thought, and took another sip. "Hmm, it tastes a little like ours but different. I like it. I think the big difference is that it's warm. Ours is always cold."

Mrs. Adams sat down at the head of the table as Johnny asked, "Did Nabby take Tommy up for a nap?"

"Yes, she took both boys up about five minutes ago." Mrs. Adams looked at Heath and Hadden. "So, boys, I want to talk to you now that we have a moment without interruption." She paused, trying to figure out how to word what she wanted to say. She tapped her fingers on the table and finally said, "As you may already know, we have been at war with Britain since April of last year. Sometimes we even hear some of the gunshots or cannons being fired here. Johnny and I witnessed a bloody battle from Penn's Hill just two months after the fighting began. We lost a dear friend in that battle."

"I told them about the Battle of Bunker Hill when we were looking at the cows."

Mrs. Adams nodded at Johnny and continued. "Well, there were a lot of men that were hurt and some of the men came here to heal and be nursed back to health again. One of the patriots was Colonel William Prescott. He was wounded and was brought here for six days. During that time we talked a little about the battle. He had said that they lost the Battle of Bunker Hill because they didn't have enough musket balls. He even told his men, 'Don't fire until you see the whites of their eyes,' because of the limited amount of ammunition they had."

"Yes, after that battle, I helped Mama and Uncle Elihu melt spoons, knives, forks, and anything else we could find to make pewter musket balls for the war."

Mrs. Adams smiled at Johnny. "Yes, I can't believe that next month will be an entire year since we lost him. Well, anyway, one night Colonel Prescott told me about one of his men, Audie Murphy. He said Audie had told him that he came from the year 1944 and was in a big war there. He said it was a World War, can you imagine such a thing?"

"It must have been World War II. My great-grandpa was in that war. He didn't talk about it much but he had a cool tattoo from when he was in it," Heath said.

Mrs. Adams raised her eyebrows. "It's true? There is to be an actual world war?" She shook her head in disappointment and sadness. "I just can't imagine such a thing. You said World War Two, meaning that there was one before that?"

"Yes. In 1921 they brought a man back that died in World War I but they don't know who he is. They made a very special place for him to be buried and placed him in it. He is the soldier that represents all of those that are unknown that died during World War I. There are two other people buried there too. They are unknowns from World War II and the Korean War," Heath explained.

"Yeah, they had a fourth one but they figured out who he was so they took him out and buried him in his hometown I guess," Hadden added.

"Yeah. The man fought in the Vietnam War. Oh, and they have a guard marching back and forth in front of the tomb protecting it all day, all night, all the time, no matter what the weather." Heath got up from the table to demonstrate. "The guard marches 21 steps." Heath marched only five steps in his demonstration. "Then he turns towards the east and bangs the heels of his shoes together, waits 21 seconds, turns and bangs his shoes again, waits another 21 seconds, then marches another 21 steps, then does it all over again all day every day." Heath sat back down. "They carry a rifle with a knife on the end of it. They always have that on the shoulder that is closest to the visitors to show that they stand between the Tomb and any threat to it."

"It sounds like they carry a bayonet. The rifle with a sword on the end of it," Johnny remarked.

As Mrs. Adams got up from the table to gather the bowls and glasses she said, "That is so sad not knowing who the person is, but it is a wonderful tribute to these unknown soldiers. I'm sure the families must be devastated not knowing what happened to them. Why is the number 21 used so often while guarding the tomb?"

"It's from the 21-gun salute. It's the highest honor anyone can receive in the military," Heath explained.

Satan got up from where he was laying in the other room and came to see if anything fell on the floor.

Hadden noticed that she placed everything in a container but there wasn't a sink to wash them in. "Where's the sink? How are you gonna clean 'em?"

"I will get water from the well and clean them in this tub after our conversation."

"Can I help? I never saw a well before."

"You never want to help Mom when she has to do the dishes. What's the difference if it's in a sink, a dishwasher, or in a tub?" Heath wanted to know.

"'Cause everything is different here. There's a well here and not a sink."

Mrs. Adams smiled at Hadden. "I would appreciate the help. Thank you, Hadden. While we are washing, you can tell me what a sink and a dishwasher are."

Hadden smiled, scrunched his nose, and stuck out his tongue at Heath.

Mrs. Adams sat down at the table again and continued with her story. "As I was saying, Audie Murphy had told Colonel Prescott that he found a cave when he was on patrol in Germany. Audie was curious and went into the cave. As he was standing there taking a moment to take in the calm, cool, and quietness of the cave, he came across a beautiful green gemstone. One as he'd never seen before."

"Maybe it's like the one I have!" Hadden exclaimed.

"We have," Heath corrected.

Mrs. Adams smiled and went on with the story. "While he was looking at the gemstone, some of his comrades came into the cave. He held it in his fist and it began to get warm."

Hadden's eyes widened. Heath turned his head to look at Hadden and then turned back to Mrs. Adams to listen with complete immersion.

Mrs. Adams noticed the look between the brothers and smiled. "He thought it was odd but was fascinated by it. Even with the noise of gunshots and cannons around, he couldn't get over the fact that this beautiful green gemstone was beginning to glow a bit and get warm in his hand. He was just mesmerized. He sat down to give it a closer look and when he leaned back to rest his back against the wall of the cave, he said he just fell through it. All of a sudden he was here in 1774."

Hadden was excited and exclaimed, "Whoa, just like we did! Only we came here in 1776."

Mrs. Adams nodded and paused for a moment. She took a sip of water. "Yes, just like you did. Colonel Prescott thought Audie was suffering from mania or something because the story was so far-fetched. He had said that Audie was here for almost a year until he met an old woman who told him what he had to do to get back home. The old woman said that he had to go back to the cave where he came to 1774 in. Only in that cave could he go back to 1944." She stopped talking for a moment to take another sip of water and to judge the boys' reactions to this outlandish tale. Johnny and Heath were on the edge of their seats, literally. Hadden sat there with his left hand under his chin and the other hand resting on his left arm while his feet were swinging back and forth. All of them were listening intently. Mrs. Adams was thinking that she couldn't believe that she was telling this story out loud to these three young boys. Then she muttered under her breath to herself, "Well, dern, I can't believe that I believe the story myself now!"

"What did you say, Ma?" Johnny asked.

"Oh, I was just muttering to myself," Mrs. Adams admitted as she waved her hand and continued. "Colonel Prescott said Audie asked for permission to leave to go to the cave. Naturally, the Colonel said no because they were in the midst of a war so, naturally, he couldn't let anyone leave. The Colonel said, 'Staff Sergeant Murphy actually thought that I would allow him to leave in the middle of a war! Can you believe that, ma'am?' My thought at that time was that his fever was so high that he was hallucinating. Now that you two have shown up with a similar experience, it makes me wonder about his story."

"What happened to Audie Murphy?" Heath questioned.

Mrs. Adams was quiet for a moment. "According to Colonel Prescott, Audie Murphy went missing the next day. The Colonel sent four men out to the cave in search of him.

Two days later the men came back and said that they saw footprints in the dirt walking to the wall of the cave, but they ended there. The only thing there besides his footprints were his gun and helmet so they brought them back. He was nowhere to be found."

Heath was so excited that he jumped off his chair and it almost fell over. "So that means someone knows how to help us get home!"

"I have to remember if Colonel Prescott mentioned this woman's name so we may find her and question her about this story." Mrs. Adams squeezed her eyes shut to try to remember. "Johnny, why don't you take Heath out and show him the grounds while Hadden and I clean up after dinner? This will give me some time to try and remember who the woman is while I have some tea for my headache."

Johnny jumped off his chair and Heath slowly slid off of his. Heath walked away with his head down.

Mrs. Adams knew he was scared and worried that he wouldn't be able to get back home. "Have no worry, Heath, we will figure this out. I am most sure of it." Heath smiled and walked out the door behind Johnny.

★ CHAPTER SEVEN ★

AFTER MRS. ADAMS FINISHED HER TEA, SHE GRABBED two buckets from the pantry directly off the kitchen. She handed one to Hadden and said, "Alright, we are all prepared to fetch water from the well." She opened the back door and led Hadden to the side of the house.

As they were walking toward the well, Hadden noticed a few pigs in a pen and some chickens running around loose. "Mrs. Adams, shouldn't those turkeys be in cages or something?"

Mrs. Adams looked over where Hadden was pointing and laughed. "Well, they are *chickens* and they always run around the yard. Later tonight, my servants will be sure that they are in their chicken coops so tomorrow we can fetch the eggs," she explained.

"So they kinda have to be tucked into bed at night?" Hadden asked with a smile.

Mrs. Adams laughed. "Yes, if they aren't in their coops at

night, we may get a fox or something that might eat them.”

“I thought chickens were just white, I didn’t know they come in different colors. I saw you had two eggs sitting in a basket on the kitchen table. Mom always puts our eggs in the fridge. One time she forgot to put the eggs away after she went shopping and she had to throw ’em all out. She says they’ll go bad if they’re left out too long. How come you leave yours out? Don’t they go bad?”

Mrs. Adams really had no idea what Hadden was talking about. She wondered what a fridge was and why you would have to put the eggs in one. “No, our eggs don’t go bad. I don’t know why your mom’s would go bad by not placing them in, what did you say, a fridge?”

“Huh. Yeah, it’s a fridge. It keeps our food cold. If I ever see my mom again, I’ll ask her why she puts the eggs in there.”

“I know you will see your mom again,” Mrs. Adams said, trying to reassure Hadden.

Hadden caught a glimpse of the well. “Ah, there it is,” he said as he ran over to a circle of stones about three feet high that surrounded a hole in the ground. On top of the well was a roof with a pole going across it and rope was wrapped around the pole.

Mrs. Adams reached over the wall and grabbed the rope. “We have to tie the bucket onto the rope and lower it into the well.” She tied her bucket’s handle with a knot and then placed it in the center of the well. “Now we turn this handle and let the bucket go down." She turned the handle counter-clockwise for about two minutes and said, "Once we hit the water, we let the bucket fill and then we pull it up like this." Mrs. Adams began turning the handle clockwise, slowly bringing the bucket of water back up. She placed the handle in a twelve o'clock position and then put a wooden peg behind the handle in a hole that was made into the stone. This way it didn't move and the bucket didn't fall back down into the well. She reached over and grabbed the bucket and lifted it up to the brick wall. "Now, can you do all that?" she asked as she untied the bucket from the rope.

"Yeah, I can do that." Mrs. Adams handed him the rope and Hadden began tying it in a knot around his bucket.

Once he pulled it tight he lifted the bucket up by the handle and was ready to toss it into the well. "Oh, wait a moment," Mrs. Adams said, reaching for the bucket. "I just want to see how well you did with the knot. We don't want to lose the bucket, yes?"

"Yeah, okay, but I know I did a good knot. I know how to tie good knots because I like to fish and if you catch a fish and you don't tie the knot right, you're gonna lose your fish. I caught a big bass one time and it stayed right on the line!" Hadden said with pride. "We have a great big bass in Culver's Cove lake named Old Lucky and everyone tries to catch him. I hope I tie my knot really, really good when I catch him!"

Mrs. Adams smiled while she was listening and checking the knot. "Well, you know what, Hadden, you are clever! This knot is perfect."

Hadden smiled and took the bucket from Mrs. Adams. He dropped it over the well and it swung back and forth a few times. He grabbed the handle getting prepared to start turning it when Mrs. Adams reminded him, "Hold it tight before you pull out the peg, otherwise it will drop all the way down and the rope may keep unwinding. We don't want that to happen."

Hadden grabbed the handle and took out the peg. He immediately felt the weight of the bucket on the end of the rope. He began turning the handle but it went up instead of down. "Oops," he said and turned it in the opposite direction, lowering the bucket.

Once Hadden had the hang of it, Mrs. Adams said, "So, tell me, where did you and Heath get your names from? It is customary here that we name our children after their ancestors. For instance, Johnny is named after his great-grandfather, my grandfather, my mother's father. Are you and Heath named after someone?"

Hadden continued to turn the handle, which seemed to be taking forever and a day. "Yeah, Heath's name came from my mom. She loves movies and —"

"Movies?" Mrs. Adams interrupted.

Hadden hesitated. "Yeah, they are, um, well..." Then his eyes lit up and he asked, "Did you ever see a play?"

"Yes."

"Well, it's like a play but it is put on some machine where you can watch it over and over again."

Mrs. Adams' eyebrows lifted and after a moment she said, "Oh. Forgive me for interrupting. I just want to understand everything."

"Yeah, no worries. I'm excited about being here a little bit because everything is so different. It must be kinda the same for you with us saying stuff like bathroom and stuff. I'm just really afraid that I will never see my mom and dad again."

"I know, dear. We will figure this out somehow. You got here, there must be a way to go back there, right?" Mrs. Adams tousled his hair and Hadden grinned. "So, Heath was named after a movie?"

"Well, Mom liked the movie *Wuthering Heights*. I think I said that right. There was a guy in it named Heathcliff so she named Heath after the guy in the movie."

Mrs. Adams clapped her hands and exclaimed, "So his full name is Heathcliff. What a very dignified name!"

"Nope, it's just Heath."

Mrs. Adams laughed, "Well, I still think it's dignified. And how did your name come about, Hadden?"

"Well, my mom said that she thought for sure that I was going to be a girl and was gonna name me Heather. But surprise! They got me instead. So my mom decided that the closest thing to Heather would be the hill that they grow on. So I'm named after a flowery hill." Hadden shook his head and rolled his eyes. "My mom said." He made his voice all squeaky trying to imitate his mom's voice. "Hadden, look at it this way, your name is a hill where beautiful flowers grow. Isn't that nice?" Then he said in his usual voice, "Ah, no. I just want to be named like all the other kids with names like Mike, Bobby, Jimmy, ya know?"

"Well, it sounds like your mother really likes this flower. I think it's a very clever name and I think you will come to love it over time."

"I dunno about that. Hey, I hit the water!"

"Wonderful! Let it down a bit more so it may fill up and then just bring the bucket back up."

Hadden let the water flow into the bucket and began turning the handle in the opposite direction to bring the bucket up. It was a bit slower this time because there was more weight on it and the well was pretty deep. After a few minutes of this Hadden asked, "Mrs. Adams, can you help me with this? I'm getting tired already. Plus I'm sweating like a big bad boon sittin' on the moon."

Mrs. Adams laughed as she stepped up to quickly help him. "Oh yes, dear." She grabbed the handle and let Hadden step aside as she continued to turn it. Then she asked, "What is a big bad boon?"

Hadden tipped his head and furrowed his brows thinking that she must know what a boon is and wondered if she was testing him. He said, "You know, it's like a monkey, but they have big red butts."

Mrs. Adams laughed so hard she actually snorted. She cupped one hand over her mouth as she laughed and she nearly let go of the handle. "Oh, you mean a baboon!" she exclaimed while still laughing.

"Yeah, that's what I said."

"No, it's ba-boon. Not bad boon," she corrected him.

Hadden studied her for a second to see if she knew what she was talking about. "Really? I thought boon was another word for monkey and those monkeys were the bad ones of the monkey family."

Mrs. Adams was feeling a little more at ease and lighthearted. Laughing helped a great deal during this stressful time. She finished turning the handle until the bucket came up. Hadden was leaning over the side of the well looking down. Mrs. Adams noticed that he was actually climbing up the wall bit by bit. "Hadden, get down from there, please. I don't want you to fall into the well. We would never see you again."

Hadden jumped off the wall and began walking with Mrs. Adams back to the house. Before they made it to the door, he noticed a little boy walking around the corner of the house.

"Oh, James, I apologize. I had forgotten our lesson for today. I have a couple of visitors from New Jersey and I got a little taken off course," Mrs. Adams said apologetically.

The boy looked to be about the same age as Hadden. He was dressed in knickers and a shirt like Hadden was wearing but the only thing that was different between this little boy and Hadden was the color of his skin. James was African American.

Mrs. Adams introduced the boys and explained to Hadden, "I have been giving James lessons in reading and writing for about a month now. He is a very clever young man."

"Thank you, Ma'am," James said with a smile.

"Come in, James. You get started in the parlor while I show Hadden how we clean our dishes. I'll be with you in a moment."

James walked in the back door and through the kitchen to the parlor.

Mrs. Adams took the bucket from Hadden and placed it next to hers on the table. She poured a little water into one washtub and a little water into another one. She took a bowl and showed Hadden just how to soak the rag, place the bowl in the water, and clean it off, then take it and place it in the next tub to rinse off any residue the soap left behind.

Hadden caught on right away. "Oh, this is easy. It's

sorta like how my mom does it. I thought it was going to be different somehow," he said with much disappointment.

Mrs. Adams smiled. "Dirty dishes are dirty dishes wherever you are. You can just leave it there and I will wash them later if you wish."

"No, I'll do them."

"Then I will let you finish while I give James his instruction for the day." She tousled Hadden's hair and joined James in the parlor.

Hadden got started on cleaning the bowls, glasses, and spoons. He was extra careful with the glasses because a lot of times he ended up breaking something. Once when he was little he decided to help Mom with the dishes. He slid the chair over to the sink, climbed up, and grabbed the sponge that she always used. He took the dish soap and poured some in the sink and turned the water on. He used cold water because he didn't want to burn himself. He placed the sponge in the sink and discovered that there were a lot more bubbles than when Mom did the dishes. He shrugged and reached for another plate and added it to the sink. The bubbles kept growing. He poured dish soap on the sponge like Mom did. Then he reached into the water and found a plate and started washing it with the sponge. When he discovered that the bubbles were now pouring over onto the floor he began to panic. He accidentally dropped the plate on the floor and it broke into several pieces. He cried because he felt so bad for breaking the plate and he was just trying to help. Mom came running into the kitchen when she heard the crash. She stood there for a minute and then just laughed. Hadden didn't understand what was so funny. When Mom was telling Dad about it later on that night she said, "He had the soapiest sponge that you ever could imagine, bubbles flowing over the sink, and a shattered plate all over the floor. I thought it was the cutest, sweetest thing! And I made it to the sink just in time to turn the water off before the water overflowed." Hadden didn't want anything like that to happen again, so he was very careful with the dishes.

When he was all through with the dishes, he dried off his hands and walked into the parlor where Mrs. Adams was teaching James how to read. She saw Hadden come into the room and waved her hand toward a chair adjacent to them. "Come sit over here, Hadden, maybe you can help me to teach James some words." She showed him a chalkboard with a few words on it. Just then they heard the sound of little feet coming down the stairs. Tommy and Charlie had woken up from their naps.

CHAPTER EIGHT

MEANWHILE, WHEN HEATH AND JOHNNY WENT OUT the back door, Satan whizzed past them, grabbed a stick, and brought it over to Johnny. "Go fetch, boy," Johnny said as he took the stick and threw it as far as he could. Satan went running off to retrieve it.

"So, what do you do around here for fun?" Heath asked.

"We play games such as chess, Parchese, marbles, tag, hide and seek, jump rope, scotch-hopper, hoops and graces, hoop racing, horseshoes, rounders, and battle-doers."

"Battle-doers and rounders sound like fun. What are those games?"

"Battle-doers is where we take a cork and hit it with our hands back and forth. The opponent gets a point when the player misses hitting the cork."

"Oh. That's like our badminton or tennis games only we use rackets instead of our hands. What is rounders?"

"Rounders is a game where we throw a ball to someone

holding a stick. There is a square and on each corner of the square is a post that we must touch after we hit—"

Heath interrupted Johnny. "That sounds like what we call baseball. When you hit the ball with the stick, which we call a bat, you run to the square, or base, trying not to be tagged out. When you touch all the squares, you get a point."

"Yes! I cannot believe that it is still played over 200 years from now."

"Yeah, I guess a lot of the games we have in 2024 started back," Heath couldn't help but laugh out loud. "I don't know if I should say back then or here," he said and laughed again. "I know what marbles, tag, hide and seek are. Scotch-hopper must be like my hopscotch. Horseshoes I know, but I never heard of the hoop games."

"We have two games with hoops. Hoop racing is where we race while rolling the large hoops with only our hands or sticks."

Heath remembered seeing kids playing with a hoop when he was still in the woods checking out the scenery. "I guess that's what the kids were playing when I came here. They had a big hoop."

"Yes, most likely so," Johnny agreed. "When I play, I prefer sticks. It is more challenging and I am very good at it," Johnny explained proudly. "In hoops and graces, competitors launch a small hoop into the air by placing it around a pair of sticks and then quickly pulling the sticks apart. The other player has to catch it with their sticks. If they drop it their opponent gains a point. A lot of the ladies play that game."

"Humph, I think I'd be good at that too. Do you wanna play hoop racing?"

"Certainly! There are hoops in the barn. Let's go get them."

Heath, Johnny, and Satan all ran to the barn to get the barrel hoops. Naturally, Satan won the race but Johnny made it to the barn before Heath did. Heath wasn't accustomed to the heat of 1776. He was used to having a break here and there with air conditioning, getting a little refreshed, and then going out again. There was no "refreshing" here. It was just hot, hot, hot all the time. They didn't even have fans!

Heath came up behind Johnny and looked around the barn. Two horse-drawn carriages loomed over them in the darkness. One had two wheels and held two people. It didn't have a roof but it had a canopy that you could open and close. Johnny said, "This is the whiskey that we talked about before. It's much smaller than the other one and only needs one horse." The other had four wheels, held four to six people, and looked about the size of Heath's dad's car. Both of them had wooden shafts that came out from the carriage so the horse could be attached.

While Heath was thoroughly checking out the carriages, Johnny found the barrel hoops. "Ah, here they are, let's go!" he exclaimed.

They walked out of the barn and made their way past the apple orchard. Johnny mentioned that the spring had been a cold one and things were three weeks behind in blooming and blossoming. He pointed over to the left where the crops in the field were only about six inches tall. "That's our cornfield. It looks very poor right now because it's been so dry."

Heath's curiosity got the best of him and he couldn't help but ask, "Do you really use corn cobs?"

Johnny couldn't figure out what he was talking about for a minute. Then he finally realized that Heath was talking about wiping your bottom and he smirked. "Yes. Why do you find that hard to believe?"

"I just can't imagine using it. We use toilet paper and it seems so much easier AND softer. We use it and then we just put it in the toilet and flush it. Then it goes down the drain." Johnny was intrigued and was going to question Heath a bit more but Heath began talking before Johnny got the chance. "Do you think your mom will be able to help me and Hadden get back home?"

Johnny saw the fear and the tension in Heath. He just couldn't imagine being in his shoes. "I think Mama will do everything in her power to help you get back home. She is the type of person that helps everyone she can and if she can't..." Johnny put his index finger on his cheek and thought for a moment. "Well, there was never a time that she couldn't help someone. I am confident that you will return to the year 2024."

"I hope you're right." Heath had the weight of the world on his shoulders and there wasn't a thing he could do about lightening the load and he felt every bit of it.

They came across a fallen tree and stopped. Johnny let the hoops fall to the ground. "I know I am. Don't worry any more about it. Now, I like to play in front of the trees here because there is a slight incline and it makes the hoops go faster, which makes the game more fun. Let's find two sticks about this long to play with." Johnny held his hands apart to show how big the sticks should be and started searching.

Heath sat down on the log and sulked. "What if I can't get back home? Where will we go? My mom and dad will be so scared. I'm so scared."

Johnny went over and sat next to Heath on the log and gave him a pat on the shoulder. "Have faith, my friend. I am certain you will go home. Mama said she just has to remember the old woman's name and I know she will! Then we shall go and find her and hopefully she will know how to see you home."

Heath looked at his feet and just nodded in agreement while still sulking.

Johnny took this opportunity to question Heath a bit about his life to take his mind off of his dilemma. "So tell me what it is like in the year 2024. Are we a free country? Free of King George?"

Heath was grateful for the subject change. At least it was something that he knew about. "Yes! I just learned all this in school this year. We learned that July Fourth is America's birthday! It's called Independence Day. We have barbeques, fireworks, and parties to celebrate."

Johnny was excited and jumped up off the log. "Golly! That's wonderful! Papa and Mama will be so happy! So it happens in July on the fourth? What year does this happen?"

Heath's eyes got real wide. "Oh my gosh! It happened in 1776! It's going to happen in a couple of days!"

"I must go to tell Mama the great news!" Johnny hollered and started running home with Satan slightly in the lead.

Heath walked slowly, deep in thought. *Wow, I just learned this year that our country will be is 248 years old. Right this very minute it hasn't even been born yet.* That just blew his mind. Once it all sank in, he started to run too.

When he got to the house, Heath found everyone gathered in the parlor along with someone he hadn't met yet. Johnny was excitedly telling Mrs. Adams what Heath had told him about America becoming free from King George and Britain in just a few more days. Mrs. Adams was stunned. She looked at Heath for confirmation and asked him, "Is this true?"

Heath nodded and smiled.

Mrs. Adams was so excited about hearing about their independence from Britain that she jumped up from her chair and said, "That's wonderful!" and started heading towards the kitchen.

Satan was even happy that everyone was happy. It was not very often lately that he saw his family so happy and excited. He got up from his resting spot next to Johnny and barked.

Mrs. Adams wanted to tell Mary the great news and ran about twenty steps but then stopped. She stood in the kitchen and thought about what might happen if she told Mary. She would most likely want to know how she knows this information. She was so excited that she felt like she could just burst at the seams with joy, but knew that she couldn't tell anyone though. She walked back into the parlor just in time to hear Hadden asking Heath a question.

"And how do you know all about that, Mr. Brainiac?"

"Doofus, it's the Fourth of July! That's what the holiday is all about! My teacher said that on July 2nd, 1776, independence from Britain was approved. It was in the newspapers and everything."

Mrs. Adams exclaimed, "That's today!"

Heath was more than happy to share the good news because it made everyone so happy. "Then they spent a couple of days redoing the wording and everyone signed it on July 4th... hmmm, what did Mrs. Becker say?" He thought for a moment. "Oh yeah, then they DECLARED it on the 4th."

"What does declared mean?" Hadden asked.

"That's why it's called the Dec-la-ration of Independence," Heath said slowly, hoping that would satisfy Hadden's inquisitiveness because he really didn't know what it meant either.

Hadden was still confused and asked again, "Okay, one more time. What does declared mean, Einstein?"

Mrs. Adams felt like she should step in at this point. She clapped her hands and explained, "Declared means that they announced it and made it official."

"Yeah, that's what it means," Heath said as he nodded.

Shy Nabby still wasn't quite comfortable with Heath, Hadden, and James around, but with this good news she was so excited that she spoke up and asked, "So does that mean the war is over?"

Everyone looked at Heath for the answer. He suddenly felt like giving all this information to them might not be a good thing. *What if it changes things for the future? I can't remember exactly how long it went on for but it didn't stop after July 4, 1776. What if I say that the war goes on for a while longer, what could happen?* Heath figured he better say something so he just said, "Um, I dunno. But the Declaration of Independence was a long list of the things that the king did to the people here. There were 27 problems listed on it. The second paragraph is the Preamble and the words are the most recognized words today, 'We hold these Truths to be self-evident, that all Men are created equal, that they are endowed by their Creator with certain unalienable Rights, that among these are Life, Liberty, and the Pursuit of Happiness.'"

"Okay, so if they announced their split from Britain there wouldn't be any reason to fight anymore. Right?" Hadden asked.

Heath wished Hadden would butt out of this conversation. He wanted to tell everyone that a lot of people died. Mrs. Becker even said that a few other countries were helping us become an independent nation. France, Spain, and the Netherlands lost a lot of people in trying to help America be free from Britain. He wanted to tell them that out of five thousand soldiers who died from Spain, four thousand of them died as prisoners on British ships just sitting in New York Harbor. A lot of people even died of disease too. The war wasn't over until the Treaty of Paris was signed. He knew that it wasn't a good idea to bombard them with so much information.

While Heath was thinking, James piped up and asked a question of his own. "How do you know all of this if it hasn't happened yet?"

Well that put a spin on things, didn't it? Heath just stood there with a blank look on his face. Hadden, of course, spoke first. "Heath's teacher told him all that in school. He just learned it. I knew some of it because when he had a test on it Mom was helping him study for it and I listened. When I get to the fifth grade, I'm gonna be smarter than all the other kids!" Everyone laughed but James was still waiting for the answer.

Mrs. Adams quickly gestured to the doorway, saying, "James, I think we better wrap up your lesson for today. Is that alright?"

James rose from the chair. "Yes, Ma'am. Should I come tomorrow at the same time?"

Mrs. Adams agreed and placed her hand on James's back and walked him to the front door. As they were walking, she could be heard telling James that he had done an excellent job painting the fence out front and that she hoped tomorrow he would be able to fix the post by the oxen barn. After James left, Mrs. Adams came back to the parlor and looked at her daughter. "Nabby, please take Tommy and Charlie outside while I talk to the boys."

"Yes, Mama." Nabby was a very bright girl and she had been watching Heath and Hadden with curiosity and suspicion. She would have to talk to Mama after supper tonight about these two boys. She turned to Tommy and said, "Come'ere Tommy," as she took Tommy's hand and helped him off the floor where he was sitting next to Satan. Then she walked towards Charlie, who hid behind his mother's leg. "Would you like to go play horseshoes, Charlie?"

Charlie quickly grabbed Nabby's hand and began pulling her towards the back door while saying, "Yes! I'll get the horseshoes out of the barn. I know where they are!"

"Nabby, just don't let Charlie over-exert himself. Even though it's been a fortnight since he recovered, he should still be cautious."

"I will, Mama."

Mrs. Adams turned to the boys and started with something Heath wasn't expecting. "Have either of you had the mumps before?"

CHAPTER NINE

HEATH WAS CAUGHT OFF GUARD WITH THE QUESTION. HE certainly wasn't expecting a question like that. "No, we get shots so we don't get diseases like that. A couple of years ago a new one started called Covid. No one was allowed anywhere and if you had to go out, you had to wear a mask. That lasted a while."

"Oh, well I'm glad that you were vaccinated for the mumps. The mumps have been going around and I would hate to have either one of you catch it. Charlie just recovered from them," Mrs. Adams explained.

"Yeah, we get shots and I hate 'em." Hadden scrunched his nose and shook his head. "One time I started screaming so much that the doctor wouldn't give it to me. So Mom took me home and told me that if I got a shot from the doctor the next day, I could use Dad's drone at the park. It has a camera and everything! But I still wouldn't so she said that if I didn't get the shot and I got the mumps, I would die. So I got the shot and got a lollipop for not screaming."

Mrs. Adams laughed and her smile stayed on her lips for a moment longer. "I'm not quite sure what a drone, a camera, or even a lollipop is but I enjoy listening to you, Hadden. You certainly are a chatterbox."

Heath sighed and rolled his eyes. "You have no idea."

Hadden wanted to be sure that Mrs. Adams knew how special controlling a drone was and said, "A drone is like a helicopter that takes pictures."

"Okay, Sir Talks-A-Lot, that still doesn't explain anything to her. Mrs. Adams still has no idea what a helicopter is either," Heath commented to Hadden. He looked at Mrs. Adams and explained, "In our time we have things called airplanes and helicopters that people sit in and make them fly around high in the sky."

Mrs. Adams' and Johnny's eyes went wide and their jaws dropped. Mrs. Adams' hands even went to her cheeks in amazement.

"Fly like a bird?" Johnny uttered in shock.

Heath smiled. "Yes, just like a bird, but it doesn't flap wings or anything. It just goes up and comes back down. A drone is like a little helicopter that we can fly in the sky using a little box while we're standing on the ground."

"How does it work? What makes it fly?" Mrs. Adams inquired.

Heath shrugged. "I dunno."

"Wow! I just can't imagine such a thing!" Johnny sighed.

Heath laughed and continued explaining what the items were that Hadden mentioned. "A camera is a box that when you hit a button on it, it grabs, um... hmmm, I don't know what word to use."

Hadden pointed to the wall. "It's like those paintings on the wall, only they aren't painted. They just come out looking like, like, like they are real. Humph." He furrowed his eyebrows and said, "I dunno either."

"Yeah, I guess what Hadden said. It just looks like they took the... Oh! It's a portrait! That's the word! They take the portrait and put it on a piece of paper like you would write a letter on."

Mrs. Adams understood but couldn't imagine what a picture from a box would look like or even how such a thing could possibly work. She was still trying to wrap her mind around the fact that people could fly like birds. After a moment she said, "And I am guessing a lollipop is something that is nice to have since it seemed to be a reward."

"Yes, it's candy on a stick." Hadden was happy to answer that one at least.

Johnny's face lit up. "Candy on a stick! What a wonderful idea! I can see how that can be a reward."

"Ya know, in all the paintings that I've seen of people around your house, they never smile. Aren't they happy?" Hadden inquired.

"Yes, we are happy," Mrs. Adams said. "When we pose for a painting it takes a long time so we don't smile and the artist just paints us the way they see us. I hope we don't look sad."

"I just wondered because no one smiles in 'em, that's all."

Heath remembered being over at his friend Bobby's house and listening to the conversation he was having with his mom about an old picture. It was sorta brownish looking and the people were wearing old looking clothes. Bobby's mom said that the camera took so long to actually take the picture that they probably got tired of smiling while they were waiting for it to flash. He'd never thought about paintings before.

Mrs. Adams sat down on the loveseat and put her hands in her lap. "Well now, we have to figure something out about this dilemma you're in. I know I can remember the name of the woman from Colonel Prescott's story given a moment to actually sit and think about it."

"Mrs. Adams, can Johnny show Hadden your orchards and corn fields and stuff while you think about it?" Heath asked.

Johnny nodded. "Yes, I think that is a good idea. I left the hoops over there when I found out about our independence."

"What were you doing with hoops? I thought only girls play with hula hoops," Hadden said teasingly.

Heath laughed. "No! It's not hula hoops. It's hoops that came off a massive barrel. We were going to play a game of hoop racing with them."

Mrs. Adams said, "That sounds like a great idea. You three go play a bit of hoop racing so I can finally have a little peace and quiet to clear my head and think."

All three boys turned around and ran out the back door. Hadden almost tripped over Satan but managed to keep his balance this time. Heath and Johnny raced over to the orchard and came upon the log where they left the hoops. Heath beat Johnny this time around. Hadden came up a second behind them. Hadden just stood there looking in the opposite direction of where Heath and Johnny were standing. "Wow, you can see so far away!"

Johnny proudly said, "Yes, we have nine and a half acres here. We have apple orchards, corn fields, wheat fields, potatoes..."

Hadden interrupted, "Okay, we get it. You have lots of fields." Heath elbowed him for being rude and Hadden knew he deserved that one so he kept quiet.

"We even have a cranberry bog!"

Hadden had no idea what that was but wanted to make up for being rude so he said, "Oh, that's cool."

Johnny smirked. "Is cool a good thing?"

Hadden and Heath laughed and both said in unison, "Yes."

Hadden tapped Heath on his shoulder. "Jinx."

Johnny looked at Hadden with a questioning look. "As you said before, you say jinx when two people say the same thing at the same time. Is this to prevent bad luck? "

Hadden raised one eyebrow and looked at Heath. Heath raised one eyebrow and looked at Hadden. They both put their hands up and said, "I dunno," at the same time. They both laughed and said, "Jinx," at the same time.

Johnny shook his head and couldn't help but laugh with them. He thought that these two were funny and interesting. He really liked them and didn't want them to go home.

As they were looking around Johnny's yard, Hadden asked, "So your dad is a farmer? I guess he had to go somewhere to get seeds and stuff for the farm. Is that why he's not here?"

"Well, Papa is a lawyer. The side door of the house, where we first entered, is his office. When he is here he has his clients go through the side door. What does your papa do?"

Hadden looked at Heath and remarked, "I have no idea. He gets dressed in the morning and just goes to work."

"You're such a dork. Dad is an architect." Heath looked at Johnny and explained, "He draws houses and buildings and then people build them the way he drew them."

"That's what Dad does? He draws all day?" Hadden said with surprise.

"Yeah, that's what he does." Then they heard Mrs. Adams yelling for them to come back to the house. "Oh, maybe she remembered the old woman's name," Heath said optimistically.

Johnny silently thought *I hope not.*

When they got back Mrs. Adams was sitting in her parlor. "I finally remembered the lady's name!" she said excitedly. "Johnny, go out into the fields and find Mr. Belcher. Ask him if he had ever heard of a woman named Mrs. Marian Hawk. I remember that Colonel Prescott had said an old woman named Mrs. Hawk, and later in the conversation he said Marian Hawk lived in South Braintree. So maybe Mr. Belcher knows of her! He's from that area."

Johnny spun around and took off so fast that Heath and Hadden were still standing there in silence. Hadden couldn't stand all the room's quietness so he decided to kill it. "Johnny said that Mr. Adams is a lawyer and his office is in the next room. It must be awesome having his dad around all the time."

Mrs. Adams smiled and thought for a moment. "Yes, I am guessing awesome is a good thing and it is a very good thing when he is working at home. Unfortunately, Mr. Adams hasn't been home in over a year and we miss him terribly."

"When is he coming back?" Hadden inquired.

"I don't know, dear. Whenever his work is completed."

Hadden felt bad for the family now that he learned Mr. Adams was hardly ever home. "I think that if my dad was always away, I would miss him very much."

Johnny ran in the back door and said excitedly. "Mr. Belcher said that he does know Mrs. Hawk! He said if you want him to take you to see her, he could when he's done feeding the cows and preparing the horses."

"That's wonderful! I really don't want Henry, our coachman, to have to take us there. Mr. Belcher knows the area like the back of his hand since he grew up there." Mrs. Adams smiled and clapped her hands, then turned to Heath and Hadden. "I want so much to sit and talk with you about what it is like in your time period, but let me get some things taken care of here so we can go to see Mrs. Hawk." Mrs. Adams went out the back door to begin looking for Mary to ask if she could stay to watch the children while she took the boys over to see Mrs. Hawk.

The boys didn't know what to do at that moment. Hadden was slouched in the chair kicking his feet when he noticed a flag hanging on the wall displayed in a nice frame. It sort of resembled the American flag that he pledged allegiance to in school, but it looked weird. It had the thirteen red and white stripes, but in the blue field where the stars should be was a white cross and a red letter X on top of the cross. "Johnny, what country are you from?" he asked.

"What! We are from right here. My ancestors were pilgrims on the Mayflower and my Papa was born in the house next door. My grandmother still lives there. I was born right here in this house. My ancestors have been here almost one hundred and fifty years now," Johnny proudly replied.

Hadden pointed to the wall where the flag hung and asked, "What country is that flag from then?"

"It's from this country, ya dork," Johnny said with a smile.

Heath and Hadden laughed. Johnny caught on to whenever the boys would call each other a dork it was because they said something silly. They didn't take offense so it must be their way of teasing each other.

Heath stepped closer to the flag on the wall so he could get a better look at it. "Johnny, this isn't like the flag that we have now. Our flag still has the red and white stripes that represent the first colonies, but now it has stars in the blue field that represent each of the states of America."

Johnny thought about that for a moment. "The states?"

Heath was so happy to be questioned because he loved history and talking about it. Without realizing it, he also wanted Hadden to be proud of him. "The colonies became states and then America got bigger and bigger when other lands were joined with us. There are fifty states now and fifty stars on our flag in the blue field. The flag went through twenty-seven changes through the years." Heath pointed to the flag on the wall. "I never saw it look like that one before."

Johnny explained. "Oh, so is that why you said that you came from the United States of America? Now I understand. The stripes on this flag are the thirteen colonies and the canton, the blue section, is the flag of our mother country, Britain."

Mrs. Adams came in and sat down on the loveseat while Johnny was explaining the flag on the wall. "Did I just overhear that our flag went through twenty-seven changes?" she asked.

"You sure did! And Heath knows all about it!" Hadden said with pride for his big brother.

Heath turned a nice little shade of red with embarrassment. "I know a little about it." He tipped his head a little lower while still looking at Mrs. Adams.

"Did I miss anything else about the flag?"

"There are fifty stars in the blue section of the flag now, one star for each state in America. Even Alaska and Hawaii are a part of America too, even though they aren't connected to us," Heath explained. "We even have a special song about the flag that became our national anthem. It's called the Star-Spangled Banner and any time it's played, we are supposed to stand and place our hand over our heart like this," Heath said as he showed her how it's done. "We even pledge allegiance to it with our hands over our hearts like this too. It goes, I pledge allegiance to the Flag of the United States of America, and to the Republic for which it stands, one Nation under God, indivisible, with liberty and justice for all."

"Oh my! That's wonderful!" Johnny exclaimed.

Heath continued, "In another year from now, on June 14, 1777, the Second Continental Congress will pass the official American flag. It will be the 13 stripes and the blue field will be 13 stars in a circle representing a new constellation. Sometime after 1900, the president at the time marked the anniversary of that decree by officially establishing June 14 as Flag Day."

Mrs. Adams was overjoyed that not only was there a song about the flag but one that made the entire country proud enough to stand and pledge allegiance to our country. She was in awe over the news. "America must be something extraordinary in the year 2024 if people stand up when the flag song is played and dedicate an entire day to the flag."

"The Star-Spangled Banner," Heath reiterated. "Yeah, my great-grandpa would say that it should be a law that we stand when it's played."

Mrs. Adams was surprised by the fact that standing for the Star-Spangled Banner wasn't done by every American by 2024. "So people have a choice whether to stand for it or not and there are some that choose not to?"

"Yeah, my great-grandpa says that it just rattles his chain that people don't realize the sacrifice people gave for the red, white, and blue." Heath tried making his voice deep like his great grandfather's. "'The Code of Laws of the United States, regarding the national anthem, was written wrong. They used the words 'should' stand instead of 'must' stand.'" Heath's voice went back to normal "It became a big tadoo the last few years. Dad says that men and women have died fighting for our rights as Americans. Standing or not standing for the Pledge of Allegiance or the Star Spangled Banner is one of those rights."

Mrs. Adams was flabbergasted. "Heath, how in the world do you remember all of this information?"

"He remembers everything! He has one of those memories that when something goes in, it doesn't come out." Hadden boasted.

"I think a lot of stuff I learn I just remember because I think it's interesting. The other stuff, I don't know," he said as he shrugged.

"I am truly amazed at your memory!" Mrs. Adams exclaimed. She stood up and clapped her hands together. "So it seems America will become a great nation to be proud of! In the year 2024, are people still coming to America from other countries?"

Heath shrugged. "I guess so. My great -grandpa used to say, 'If you come to America and try to change it to the country you just left, then go back to the country that you came from.' So, yeah, I guess so."

Heath smiled thinking of his great-grandfather and one memory in particular. "Remember Grandpa's tattoo that he had from the scar he got in World War II?" he asked Hadden.

Hadden nodded and looked toward Mrs. Adams. "Yeah, he got hit with shrapnel, and out of the scar he got a tattoo. He had an eagle with one claw on an anchor and another one on an American shield with USN over top of it in funny letters. The USN is for the United States Navy and the anchor is because the Navy is always protecting our seas. The eagle is our national bird. The eagle symbolizes patriotism and unity during times of war."

Mrs. Adams gasped. "The Navy is STILL protecting our seas in 2024? I will have to tell John! It's only been eight months since it was established! And we have a national bird?"

Johnny said, "That's a great symbol for our country! Eagles are magnificent."

Mrs. Adams was amazed by all this information and beyond proud. At that moment, she felt like her heart could just burst. She just couldn't wait to write to John about all this but knew she and Johnny had to keep this to themselves for the time being. "Johnny, I know we don't keep secrets, but I think that we shouldn't tell anyone that Heath and Hadden come from a different time period. I don't think people would understand." She smirked and added, "Well, they probably wouldn't believe us either."

Johnny nodded his head in agreement, "Yes, Mama, I agree."

⋆ CHAPTER TEN ⋆

MRS. ADAMS EXPLAINED, "NOW, MARY WILL BE STAYING here with Nabby and the boys, and Mr. Belcher will drive us to Mrs. Hawk's. Mr. Belcher says that it's about a forty-five-minute ride there. Therefore, all three of you try to use the privy before we leave. I don't want to have to stop on the way."

Heath started laughing.

Mrs. Adams placed her hands on her hips and asked, "May I ask what is so funny?"

"You sound just like my mom before we go on a long ride."

Mrs. Adams smiled. "I guess a mom is a mom no matter what time period you are in," she said as she gently tousled his hair. "Now, you three get going."

"I'll race you!" Johnny called out as he took off running towards the back door. Heath ran after and Hadden followed.

The race was a close one between Heath and Johnny, but Johnny touched the side of the privy first by a millisecond.

"You know, I'm not quite sure which one of us won so let's call it a tie," Heath said.

Johnny agreed. They turned around to see Hadden standing about thirty feet away looking at something. Johnny and Heath walked over to see what caught his attention. "What are you looking at?" Johnny asked.

"I was just looking out in your front yard. Ya know, I really like this place," Hadden declared.

"Thank you," Johnny proudly said with a smile.

Heath looked around and admired the view with Hadden, "Yeah, I know whatcha mean, jelly bean. They don't have streets like we do because they don't have cars so it's just dirt for the horses and carriages. They don't have phones and electrical lines running down the streets disturbing the view. It really does look nice here. Plus it's very peaceful."

Heath saw Nabby with Tommy and Charlie in the front of the house talking with two other people. Nabby waved at them and all three boys waved back.

"Well, we better use the privy and get going before Mama wonders what happened to us," Johnny said.

When all the boys were done with their business they started their walk back to the house. Along the way, Heath and Hadden saw a man bringing two horses out of the barn. "Oooh, look! Horses!" Hadden shouted enthusiastically.

Johnny laughed.

"Gosh, you act like you never saw a horse before," Heath said sarcastically.

"I never saw a real one up close. Have you?"

Heath stopped walking. He thought for a moment, sticking his tongue out slightly to help him think. Finally, he raised his forefinger up and exclaimed, "Yes! In the Memorial Day parade down Main Street."

"Memorial Day? What is that?" Johnny asked.

Hadden quickly said, "Memorial Day is the unofficial start of summer and time for barbecues."

"No, it's not!" Heath snapped. "It's not a day to celebrate! My teacher says it's a day to honor the people who fought in the military and died while doing it. People dying isn't something to be celebrated! Veterans Day is to honor all the people who served in the military in the past and are still alive, and Armed Forces Day is to honor those who are serving now."

Johnny nodded. "Oh my, I have so many questions right now. I'll start with if you don't use horses, how do you travel?"

Hadden was quick with the answer. "We have cars."

Heath jumped in to answer the next question he knew was coming. "Cars are like your carriages, I guess, but they don't need horses to make it go. They have motors in them." Then he rolled his eyes at himself when he realized Johnny wouldn't know what a motor was. "Motors are the things that replaced the horses! Yeah, that's it! Motors have all kinds of stuff in them that make things move and it all works together to make the car go!" Heath was so stinkin' proud of himself at that moment for such an awesome answer that he couldn't help but smile.

Johnny thought for a moment about what Heath had said. "Is the military the men that fight for America?"

"Yes, and it's not just men. My friend's mom hasn't been home for a year now. He misses her so much. They are scared because they don't know where she is or what she's doing. They just pray she comes home again," Heath explained.

"So women are in the military? I thought you meant that the military are the ones that go out and fight with muskets, rifles, and cannons," Johnny said.

Heath and Hadden were a little thrown off and didn't say anything for a moment. Heath suddenly realized Johnny didn't know what women were capable of in 2024. All he knew was that the men fight and the women stay home in 1776. "Well, first, muskets and cannons aren't used any-more. We now have guns, tanks, planes, and bombs. Second, yes, women are allowed to be in the military just like men."

Johnny took a moment to absorb the information. He started walking again with his head down and his hands behind his back. Heath and Hadden walked on either side of him, and a few moments later Johnny asked, "So, these motors. Do they make the planes fly?"

Hadden jumped in. "Yes, motors make anything go!"

"So a motor can essentially make anything move?"

Hadden let that one pass to Heath.

Heath nodded. "Yeah, pretty much. I guess."

All three walked the rest of the way to the house in silence. Johnny was doing some serious thinking about how motors worked. He was fascinated with science and the thought of flying. Before he knew it, they were walking into the kitchen.

Mrs. Adams was talking with the man that was previously taking the horses out of the barn. She turned to the boys when she heard them come in. "Heath. Hadden. This is Mr. Belcher. He helps me with the farm. He is going to take us to see Mrs. Hawk. Mr. Belcher, this is Hadden and Heath... Oh, I just realized that I don't know your last name," she said looking at the boys for an answer.

"Hampton," replied Heath.

Mr. Belcher was a tall burly Black man with a soft roundness to him. He was wearing brown pants with suspenders and a white shirt. He didn't look muscular but you could tell that he was strong. "Well, I am pleased to meet you," he said as he held out his hand to give Heath a handshake. Heath took his hand and gave it a good grip and one good shake.

Hadden watched Heath and remembered Dad always said when you give a handshake always grip the person's hand tight and firm. When Mr. Belcher turned to Hadden, his hand was already out and ready to go. Mr. Belcher put his hand in Hadden's and Hadden gripped it as tight as he could and gave it one good shake. Mr. Belcher smiled and said, "That's one mighty fine handshake there." Hadden looked at Heath and smiled. Heath was proud of his little brother but probably not as proud as Hadden was of himself at that moment.

"Are the horses fastened and are we prepared to leave now?" Mrs. Adams asked Mr. Belcher.

"Yes, ready whenever you are, ma'am."

"Very good. Would you be good enough to help Johnny and Heath into the carriage now?" Then she turned to Hadden and said, "Hadden, please wait a moment, would you, dear?"

Mrs. Adams waited for Mr. Belcher to leave with Johnny and Heath. She bent down to be eye level with Hadden. "Now, I think we should be very careful about not letting it slip that you are from 2024. Do you agree?"

"Ooh, yeah. It is kinda weird, huh? I won't say anything."

Mrs. Adams smiled. "Yes, it is. It's very weird indeed." She stood up and tousled his hair. "Okay, let's go see Mrs. Hawk and hope she knows something about Audie Murphy and how to get you home."

They went out the front door and Hadden immediately ran over to the horses. "Whoa, look at the size of him! Can I pet him?"

Mrs. Adams steered him away. "How about we go see Mrs. Hawk first and then you can help Mr. Belcher with the horses when we come back? Is that alright, Mr. Belcher?"

"Oh, yes ma'am. I could use a couple of good hands to help me after we come back," he said, smiling.

Mrs. Adams looked back at Hadden. "How does that sound?"

"It sounds pretty darn good to me," Hadden said as he walked around to the door of the carriage.

The carriage sat on four wheels, two large wheels in the back and two smaller ones in the front. It had a flat top with a back that rounded out at the bottom. The front seat was on the outside of the carriage for the driver, and two long shafts attached the horses to the carriage. There were two seats inside on either side of the door. The seats were padded, and covered with a velvety maroon material, and each sat two people comfortably.

"Wow! It looks sorta like what Cinderella rode in on the way to the ball!" Hadden exclaimed.

Heath face-palmed his forehead and shook his head at what Hadden had just said. Mr. Belcher was standing at the door of the carriage waiting to help Hadden up. One of his eyebrows lifted in wonder at what he was talking about although he didn't say anything. He took Hadden's hand and helped him as he placed his foot on the step to get into the carriage.

"It's a good thing you're here to help me get into this thing 'cause I'd probably fall and break something. At least that's what Heath always says. Right, Heath?"

Heath was sitting on the furthest seat and nodded while rolling his eyes, "Yeeeees" as Hadden came in and sat next to him.

Mrs. Adams stepped up with Mr. Belcher's help. "Thank you, Mr. Belcher."

"You're welcome, ma'am." He walked to the front of the carriage and jumped up onto the driver's seat.

Johnny sat next to his mother right behind Mr. Belcher's seat. Since they couldn't talk about what the future was like because Mr. Belcher may hear and think that they had all gone mad, Mrs. Adams thought it best to talk of something current that is of interest to nine-to eleven-year-old boys. "Johnny, why don't you tell Heath and Hadden what story you finished reading last week?"

"Oh yes! Have you ever read *Gulliver's Travels*? It was a very interesting book."

Hadden jumped in the conversation with excitement. "Yes! I saw the movie!" Heath closed his eyes and shook his head at Hadden's statement but Hadden was oblivious to it and continued talking. "It was so weird how all the little people of Lilliput were only this big." Hadden put his two hands up and held them apart about six inches to show Johnny the size of the Lilliputians. "Then when he peed on the fire and was sentenced to blindness..." Suddenly Hadden became aware that Mr. Belcher could be listening in on the conversation and wondered if he had said anything that he shouldn't have. He realized that they probably wouldn't know what a movie was. He looked at Mrs. Adams and whispered, "I'm sorry."

She smiled and leaned forward to whisper, "That's alright, dear," and patted his knee.

Hadden decided he wasn't going to talk anymore.

"Yes, I agree. I thought the people of Lilliput were just nonsensical little creatures," she said and smiled at Hadden.

Heath began to worry about meeting Mrs. Hawk. He thought, *What if Mrs. Hawk doesn't know anything at all? What if I'm stuck here forever? What if I never see Mom and Dad again?* Tears began to form in his eyes and he quickly turned all the way to the left so no one could see and wiped them away.

Mrs. Adams looked around at the view and sadly said, "It's too bad it's been such a dry start to summer. Everything should look so much better than it does right now."

"Yes, the bog is even getting a bit dry," Johnny added.

Hadden couldn't help himself and asked, "What is the bog? It sounds creepy."

Johnny laughed at Hadden's statement. By the way he said creepy, he knew it meant scary. "The bog is our cranberry bog where we grow cranberries."

"Oh, why is it called a bog? Why isn't it called, like, a field or something like that?"

"Bogs are different because you don't grow cranberries in regular soil. They grow in peat moss and sand and it's very wet," Mrs. Adams explained.

"Oh, and what do cranberries taste like?"

"Don't they have cranberries where you come from?" Johnny inquired.

Hadden shrugged and then tapped Heath with the back of his hand on his chest. "Did you ever have any cranberries? Do you know what they taste like?"

Heath regained his composure and looked at Hadden. "It's what cranberry sauce is made out of, knucklehead."

Hadden's face lit up. "Oh, that's what cranberries taste like. I like them. We always have that for Thanksgiving and Christmas."

Mrs. Adams looked at Hadden and he froze, thinking he'd said something wrong again. But Mrs. Adams asked, "Is knucklehead your nickname?"

All three boys started to laugh. "Mama, I think a knucklehead is a frivolous person."

Mrs. Adams said, "Oh my!" and laughed.

After everyone was done laughing there was a quiet pause between conversations. Everyone was in his or her own thoughts.

Hadden worried about getting home for about two minutes but then thought about Conor Kingsley. Boy, was he a pain in the butt. He was so glad Conor wasn't here. It would be even worse if he were stuck here with him. "Johnny, do you have bullies here?"

Johnny tilted his head a bit, wondering what a bully was.

Heath knew immediately what that look was for and explained. "A bully is a mean person who tries to make you feel bad. They say mean things or do mean things to you."

Mrs. Adams' hand went up to her chest and her face had the look of utter surprise. "Oh my, I should hope not!" she cried.

Johnny exclaimed, "No! Sometimes we tease a little like you calling each other knuckleheads but that's about it. We wouldn't want to hurt someone's feelings on purpose. That's just wrong."

Mrs. Adams said, "I imagine that it gives them a sense of superiority or they are just miserable people that try to make others feel bad too. That's such a shame people would be like that. I feel sorry for them actually. I'm sure they are unhappy people trying to make more unhappy people. Happy people don't hurt others."

Johnny's face lit up. He sucked in a deep breath and with the exhale he declared, "Wait a moment! Yes! I believe that six or seven years ago some men were, ah..." He had to think of the word Hadden used. "Were bullying a British soldier in Boston. They were calling him names and..."

Mrs. Adams cleared her throat while giving Johnny the look. Johnny stopped talking immediately.

Heath and Hadden knew what just happened. Even 248 years ago moms were giving their kids "the look." Heath said, "I'd really like to hear about it if you don't mind."

Mrs. Adams thought for a moment. She realized that the story was most likely going to be taught through the years. So she may as well let Johnny tell it. Who knows, Heath's teacher may have even taught him about it already. She gave in and said, "Alright, Johnny, you may finish the story."

"The people in Boston gathered around a British soldier and began calling him names," Johnny began.

Mrs. Adams interrupted him. "Wait a moment, Johnny. I don't think Heath and Hadden know how bad things were between the soldiers and civilians. First, there was a war called the Seven Years' War which cost Great Britain a lot of money to fight. King George tried to recover the money he spent on the war so he placed a tax on paper, paints, glass, lead, and tea. When he did that, people in the colonies got very angry. They certainly didn't want to pay tax for stuff being sent over from their old country where no one was sticking up for them. In other words, America didn't have any representatives in Britain so it was not fair for them to put a tax on everything that Britain was sending over here."

"That's where they got the saying 'no taxation without representation,' right?" Heath asked.

"Yes! That's exactly where it came from, Heath, very good. Since it wasn't fair for all the taxes on us, we wouldn't let the British ships come and drop anything off from Britain. All of this caused a lot of tension between the British soldiers and civilians. With tempers already so high, any little thing could set anyone off and that is exactly what happened. Now I'll let Johnny tell you the rest of the story."

"Well, on March 5, 1770, a thirteen-year-old boy from the colonies, named Edward Garrick came upon Captain-Lieutenant John Goldfinch of the British Army. Edward started to tease the Captain-Lieutenant and threw snowballs at him. Another British soldier, Private Hugh White, heard what was going on and went over to help Captain Goldfinch. Edward started insulting him and poked him in the chest. Naturally, Private White got angry and hit Edward in the head with his musket. A large crowd had gathered to stand up for Edward. A fight erupted and about seven more soldiers came out to help Captain Goldfinch and Private White, but there were hundreds of colonists throwing stones, ice, and snowballs at them. They even hit them with clubs!" Johnny exclaimed. "Then the soldiers began firing their weapons at the mob of people. They killed five people. All because Edward was bullying the Captain-Lieutenant."

Heath and Hadden were shocked.

Heath said, "Wow, I hope they were sent to prison."

"Oh! No!" Johnny exclaimed and looked at his mom. "Mama, tell them what Papa did."

Heath and Hadden couldn't wait to hear what she had to say.

"Well, since they were British soldiers, no lawyer would represent them. Well, all except one." Mrs. Adams stated.

"Yes! My pa!" Johnny exclaimed proudly.

Mrs. Adams smiled at Johnny and continued, "Yes, Papa. Mr. Adams believes in the law and puts his personal beliefs aside to defend it. He believes that no person should be denied the right to counsel and a fair trial. Since tempers were heightened, the trials were delayed so that people could cool down. Eight soldiers, one officer, and four colonists were charged with murder." She paused for a moment and took a deep breath. "They began the trial for the British commander, Captain Thomas Preston, the boss of all the soldiers. It was thought that he gave the order to fire upon the mob of colonists so he was charged. Mr. Adams represented Captain Preston in court and did such a fine job that he was acquitted."

"Does that mean he went to jail?" Hadden asked.

"No, there wasn't any proof that Captain Preston had ordered the soldiers to fire into the mob of colonists so they let him go," Mrs. Adams explained.

"Ooh," Heath and Hadden both said in unison. Mrs. Adams could hear their disappointment.

"So what happened to the rest of them?" Heath asked.

"Well six of the soldiers were also acquitted, but the two that fired directly into the crowd were convicted of manslaughter."

Heath and Hadden sat back in their seats and were silent while they absorbed the story.

"After Papa helped them win, his law office got very busy," Johnny said with a smile. He was very proud of his dad.

Mrs. Adams was just as proud of him too. She admired his morals, values, convictions, and humanitarianism. She just silently wished her husband didn't have to be known as the defense lawyer for the Boston Massacre.

⭐ CHAPTER ELEVEN ⭐

MR. BELCHER ANNOUNCED THAT THEY HAD ARRIVED AT Mrs. Hawk's home as they pulled up to a stately white colonial house with a black front door. It was bigger than Johnny's house and had four white pillars in the front.

Hadden thought the pillars made the house look fancy. "Whoa, look at this place! She's gotta be loaded, for sure!"

Heath nudged Hadden to quiet down and Hadden nudged him back, which led to a nudging match.

Mr. Belcher got down from his seat and came around to open the door of the carriage to help everyone out.

"Thank you, Mr. Belcher," Mrs. Adams said as she grabbed his hand and stepped down. She walked up to the front porch as all three boys got out of the carriage.

Hadden completely missed the step. He was hanging from Mr. Belcher's hand and swinging on a slant with his other hand sweeping the ground. "Whoa, thanks a lot, Mr.

Belcher! I'd hate to break something while I'm here in 1776. My mom would kill me."

Mr. Belcher smiled and said, "You are quite welcome, young man," as he pulled the boy up onto his feet.

Heath, shaking his head, stepped down from the carriage and slowly walked to the door with Hadden while Mr. Belcher jumped into the carriage to wait until their visit was over.

Johnny was already at the front door with his mom. She knocked on the door, took a deep breath, and said a little prayer.

On the way up the walkway, Hadden whispered, "I'm scared. What if she doesn't know how to help us?"

"I'm scared too, but I know that we will get home somehow. I got good vibes about it. Trust me," Heath whispered back and smiled hoping to help Hadden feel a little better.

"Okay, but I hope your good vibes isn't just gas," Hadden said with a slight grin.

They were standing on the porch with Mrs. Adams and Johnny when the front door opened. A tall young woman stood at the door to greet them. She wore her hair pulled back into a tight bun and her dark brown skin glistened as the sun crept in through the doorway. She wore an apron for cleaning and had a gentle and cheerful voice. "Yes, may I help you?"

"I am looking for Mrs. Hawk," Mrs. Adams replied.

The young lady stepped back a bit and opened the door a little wider. In the foyer, Mrs. Adams could see an elderly woman walking towards them. The lady was average height, had blue eyes, and her gray hair was wrapped in a bun, and around her slender neck was a beautiful ruby necklace. Although she appeared to be in her seventies, her smooth and graceful walk made her seem much younger, and she seemed to radiate a very positive energy.

"Holla, are you Mrs. Hawk?" Mrs. Adams asked.

"Yes, I am. How may I help you?" she asked as she approached the front door. Mrs. Hawk looked at Johnny and smiled. Her smile quickly faded and a look of surprised recognition covered her face as she looked at Heath and Hadden. She looked past them and saw Mr. Belcher sitting in the carriage. She nodded to Mr. Belcher.

"My name is Abigail Adams and this is my son, Johnny. We are from North Braintree. These two lads are Johnny's friends, Heath and Hadden Hampton. I am wondering if I may speak with you a moment about a man that you may know by the name of Audie Murphy. I don't know much more about him other than he was a soldier in the Battle of Bunker Hill and..." She paused because she didn't know if she should say anything more at the moment.

Mrs. Hawk waved for them to enter. "Sure, sure. Come in, come in. Let's go into the parlor and talk." Then she yelled,

"Sophia, would you please bring my guests some lemonade and cookies?"

The woman that opened the door came into the room. "Yes ma'am, it will only be a minute." She smiled at Mrs. Adams and the boys, then disappeared around the corner as fast as she appeared.

They entered a large room with windows that went almost to the top of the wall. Beautiful beige curtains touched the floor. The white sheer curtains underneath the beige ones had roses in them. A rocking chair sat directly in front of a coffee table and on either side of the coffee table were two beige couches. All of this sat on a beautiful beige and burgundy rug and was directly in front of a fireplace. Above the fireplace was a portrait of a young woman sitting down, a man standing next to her, a little boy in front of the man but on the side of the woman, and a baby on the woman's lap.

Mrs. Hawk sat down in the rocking chair and waved her hand towards the two sofas on either side of the coffee table. "Please have a seat and make yourselves comfortable."

Sophia appeared with a tray of cookies, five glasses, and a pitcher of lemonade. While she balanced the tray of cookies with one hand and the corner of the cherry oak serving table, she moved the tea set that was in the middle of the table to the side of it to make room. The tea set had pretty purple flowers on all twelve of the tea cups, saucers, teapot, sugar bowl, and creamer.

"This is Sophia. She helps me around the house." Sophia smiled at them and brought the glasses over to the coffee table for each of them. "Being an old, single woman nowadays isn't so easy all by yourself. When my husband James died, I needed all the help I can get and Sophia is a great help to me. Her mama, Daisy, is my best friend. We have been friends since we were about five years old. They live in the house in the backyard that James built about 40 years ago. They are part of my family and I consider Sophia a niece of mine. Oh my heavens. Look at me. I can be such a chatterbox sometimes."

Hadden smiled and said, "That's what some people say about me! I think there's a lot of good stuff that needs to be said sometimes. Don't you Mrs. Hawk?"

Mrs. Hawk and Mrs. Adams laughed. "You are absolutely correct, young man. I couldn't agree more," Mrs. Hawk said with a wink.

Hadden looked at the cookies and lemonade. As much as he wanted to take a sip, he knew how he was with glass. There was a pretty good chance an accident was bound to happen. "I'm not going to have any of the lemonade because it's in a big glass and I don't want to break it."

"Oh, don't you worry about breaking it, dear. It's just a thing and things are not that special. People are special and you should enjoy all the good things in life while you have a life to enjoy them. If it breaks, so what. It's just a thing," Mrs. Hawk declared. Hadden liked her from that moment on.

Mrs. Adams cleared her throat and slid her hands over her thighs as she prepared to tell Mrs. Hawk the story. "Mrs. Hawk, before I ask you what I would like to ask you about, I just want you to know that I am not a frivolous person. I tell you that because what I am going to ask you will make me sound as if I am manic or a lunatic. But rest assured that I am not."

Mrs. Hawk wasn't listening with one hundred percent attention. She was thinking, *Hmm, this is quite the pickle. I thought I had at least five more years before Heath was old enough to activate the stones. Apparently, age isn't a factor. I wonder if he is showing any of his ancestors' powers? Hmm, I wonder if Abigail and Johnny know that they are time travelers; and if they do, I don't know how this is going to affect the future. Yes, it's quite the pickle.*

"You see, my son, Johnny..." Mrs. Adams paused for a moment. She was talking while she was thinking and her thinking was coming a bit slow. "You see, he was wandering in the woods when he came upon Heath and Hadden." She looked over at the boys. "They were lost in the woods and Johnny thought it best..." Mrs. Adams paused once more. "To bring them to our home to ask for my help in...helping... them...to..."

Mrs. Hawk thought, *I wish she'd get on with it and tell me how they got here already. I'm not getting any younger.* She held up her right hand interrupting Mrs. Adams. "Now, dear. I'm an old woman and I don't know how much time the good Lord has given me to be on this earth. So please stop trying to find the right words so you don't sound like a maniac and just spit them out while I'm still alive to hear them," she said with a grin.

Heath really liked Mrs. Hawk and couldn't figure out why. Hadden just grew to adore her more with each passing moment. Johnny was a little surprised that his mom was a little tongue-tied. It was not like her at all.

"I'm terribly sorry," said Mrs. Adams. "It's just that it's such a strange story and remarkable that..."

Yes, it is very strange to say the least. And if a woman such as Abigail Adams is tongue tied, then she and Johnny definitely know the boys are traveling through time. Mrs. Hawk held up her hand once again. "Wait a moment, dear. Let me stop you there. I understand that you are an intelligent, logical woman and that is why you are struggling with the words to tell me that Heath and Hadden aren't supposed to be here. I have been around a long time and have seen things that you would find unimaginable. So I can understand why you are perplexed."

"I appreciate you saying that but Heath and Hadden aren't from around here," Mrs. Adams interrupted.

"Yes, that I know. When I said 'not supposed to be here' I didn't mean here in Massachusetts, I meant here in 1776."

All four of Mrs. Hawk's guests were gobsmacked and sat

there with their mouths agape, looking at the old woman. She smiled and said, "I see you are all in somewhat of a shock over my statement. Maybe even a little relieved that I may be of some help to these two fine young men." She turned to Heath and Hadden and asked, "Now, can you tell me what happened? How did you get here?"

Hadden reached for a cookie, sat back, and waited for Heath to tell the story. He took a bite of the cookie and by the time he swallowed he realized that Heath wasn't going to say anything. Heath was still in shock with his mouth open. Hadden couldn't let the silence keep going, it was just rude, so when he finished the next bite of his cookie he said, "Well, since Heath is trying to catch flies, I'll tell ya, Mrs. Hawk. We're from 2024 and we were in this cave when Heath found a pretty green gemstone. I wanted to see it and he gave it to me to look at it, but then he wanted it back..."

Mrs. Hawk thought, *So, Audie must have dropped the emerald during his flip back to his time. Excellent! Now I just need to find the other stones that go into Georg's staff. I wish I could say something more to them now, but the boys probably need some time to absorb this time travel and all before I go and tell them what their destiny is and who I am. It's too much for such young boys to absorb.* Mrs. Hawk held up her index finger. "Okay, I think I know where this is going. You held the emerald in your hand. Did it get warm as you were holding it?"

Hadden nodded enthusiastically.

"While the emerald was warming up, did you touch the wall of the cave?"

Everyone's eyes got wider and Hadden said, "Yes! How do you know?"

Mrs. Hawk laughed at their reaction. "Well, I have heard some stories over the years. One of them, as you know, is of a time traveler named Audie Murphy." *Hmm, Heath is just like him now that I think about it,* she thought.

"And you believed him? You didn't think he was crazy?" Hadden asked.

"Well, I had to ask him a few questions before I believed his story. That's why I believe yours. Where is the emerald that you found in the cave?"

"It's in my pocket," Hadden answered.

"May I see it?"

"Well, I don't have any pockets in these things." Hadden pulled at the sides of the knickers that he was wearing. "I left it in my shorts pocket in Nabby's bedroom in your house," he said, glancing over at Mrs. Adams.

"That is not Nabby's bedchamber. It is my bedchamber that I share with Tommy and Charlie!" cried Johnny.

"Oh, me and Heath thought that it was Nabby's bed because of the curtains on it. We thought it was a little weird that you would keep your clothes in your sister's room."

Johnny folded his arms across his chest. He was insulted

that they thought his bedchamber looked like a girl's room. "Everyone's bed has curtains to contain the heat while you sleep in the winter. If you don't have curtains around your bed how do you stay warm throughout the night in the winter months?"

Hadden didn't have a complete understanding of how the heat and air conditioning in their house worked but it seemed simple enough. "We have a box on the wall that my mom or dad turns the heat on with. Then the whole house gets warm in the winter. In the summer they use the box to turn the air conditioner on and it gets cooler."

Mrs. Adams and Johnny looked surprised at the idea of a box on the wall heating and cooling the entire house.

Heath finally got over the shock that Mrs. Hawk knew that they were not from 1776 without even being told. *She just KNEW!*, he thought. "It's not just a box on the wall that does all that. There is a heater and an air conditioner that the box on the wall is hooked up to."

Mrs. Adams said, "Well, if this box warms the house and air conditions it, there must be more to it than a young lad can explain, I'm sure. But what is wrong with the air that you need to condition it?"

Hadden palmed his forehead. "Oh yeah, you don't know about that. There's nothing wrong with it. The air conditioner is the machine that makes the house cold in the summer."

Mrs. Hawk said, "Well, I would love to find out more about this heating and air conditioning, but we have to get you back to your own time." She leaned forward in her chair and asked, "Now, when was it exactly that you came here?"

"Today," said Heath. "Around lunch time I guess."

Mrs. Hawk clapped her hands and smiled. "Good. Good." She thought, *Excellent! They haven't been here long enough to really change things in the future.* "That's very good! You see, the emerald is what enabled you to travel through time. There is something very special about that emerald, more special than being a trapiche emerald."

"I have been so worried about trying to figure out how to get them home again, I forgot to ask to see the emerald for myself. What is a trapiche emerald?" Mrs. Adams asked.

Mrs. Hawk sat back and thought for a moment about the best way to explain it to her. "Well, I don't know how familiar you are with how emeralds are formed. When they form, the crystals mold into a hexagonal formation. A trapiche gemstone does the same thing but the difference is that when it is formed, black mudstones, which contain organic matter called shales, enter into the mix. The impurities fill in the crystal junctions and create a six-point radial pattern. It looks like spokes on a wheel but I think it makes the emerald look like a flower."

"It sounds beautiful," Mrs. Adams said.

Heath nodded. "It is really pretty. I can't wait to give it to my mom when I get home. I think she will really like it."

Mrs. Hawk grabbed a cookie then sat back in her chair and popped the whole thing in her mouth. She chewed it as she wiped the corners of her mouth. "I think Sophia makes the best dern cookies I've ever tasted. Mmmm mmm. Don't be afraid to take as many as you'd like." She leaned forward and pushed the tray of cookies towards the boys.

"Thank you Mrs. Hawk," Hadden said as he reached for a cookie. "Ya know what? I think that the lady in the picture over there–" Hadden pointed to the painting above the fireplace– "looks just like my grandmother." Hadden turned his head to look at Heath. "Don't you think so, Heath?"

Heath looked at the painting and suddenly stopped chewing his cookie. "Holy shells on a peanut, it does look like MomMom!" he said with his mouth full.

"Well, your grandmother must be a real looker, huh?" Mrs. Hawk said with a wink and a smile. "That is a painting of my late husband, children, and me when I was much younger. Okay, let's get back to business. Now, when I was a child I heard stories about a special emerald that is triggered when it gets warmed up by those of a certain bloodline. Apparently, you two are from that bloodline."

Hadden said, "Yeah, I was holding it for a minute, looking at it between my fingers for the light to shine through it but it didn't get warm until I held it in my fist."

Now it was Mrs. Hawk's turn to be gobsmacked. *Hadden was the one to activate it!? Oh my, I guess it is just a familial link and not the age that matters. I should have figured that both of them would have the power since both of them are the descendants of such powerful sorcerers.* Finally she said, "Yes, that explains what activated it, and Heath must have been touching you somehow for both of you to be here together. Otherwise, Hadden, you would have moved through time all by yourself."

"Yeah, we were fighting over it and we just kinda wrestled our way over here into 1776," Heath replied.

"I'm glad we did though. I wouldn't want to be here without Heath." Hadden gave his brother a little smile.

"Ah, well there you have it. In order to get back to your time again—which is what year, dear?"

"2024," Heath answered.

"It doesn't really matter though. I was just curious." *And amazed how fast time flew by.*

"Don't you know curiosity killed the cat?" Hadden said jokingly.

"But, satisfaction brought him back," Heath and Mrs. Hawk said in unison. Everyone laughed and Mrs. Hawk quickly said, "Jinx," which made Heath and Hadden laugh and shocked Mrs. Adams and Johnny. They never heard much of the word before the boys came to visit. Heath and Hadden liked her even more.

"You both must go back to that cave, hold the emerald tight so your hand generates heat to warm it up to activate it, and then you must hold hands when you go through the portal. Once you feel it get warm, it may even glow a little, only then can you walk back through the wall and go back into your dimension of time."

"Dimension? Isn't that what old people get and they don't remember stuff?" Hadden asked.

Mrs. Hawk smiled. "No dear, you are thinking of dementia. I am talking about a different dimension of time."

Hadden's eyebrows were raised as he nodded his head and said, "Oooh," like he knew what she was talking about.

Mrs. Adams had no idea what they were talking about either. Dimensions, dementia. Her head was bothering her before but now it really began to hurt. She started to rub her temples.

Mrs. Hawk looked at Mrs. Adams. "Are you alright, dear?"

"I have the beginnings of a migraine again, I'm afraid. But yes, I'll be alright. Thank you."

"I have something that may help you with that. I picked it up along my journeys some time ago." Mrs. Hawk called for Sophia and asked her to bring Mrs. Adams two of the tablets she kept in the kitchen cabinet.

Mrs. Adams felt like she was already imposing on this nice woman. "That's alright. I'm sure it will pass soon. At least I hope so anyway. I don't want to bother you, Mrs. Hawk."

"Nonsense. It's no bother." Mrs. Hawk said kindly. "You

have to be going soon so you can get Heath and Hadden back to the cave before it gets dark. You don't want to be walking through the woods to and from the cave in the dark, and with a migraine on top of it." She looked towards the door again and hollered, "Sophia, what time is it, dear?"

Sophia came around the corner. "It is now five o'clock. Would you like to have them stay for dinner, Ma'am?" She handed Mrs. Adams two little round white pills.

Mrs. Hawk stood up from her chair. "I truly wish they could, but they have an important appointment so they must be leaving. Abigail, swallow those with a drink of lemonade and in about twenty minutes you should be feeling better."

Mrs. Adams was unsure of this. She always tried a soothing tea to calm down her headache. She was a bit apprehensive about taking the little white pills.

Mrs. Hawk felt Mrs. Adams' apprehension and said, "I promise that those two little tablets will help with your migraine. It is not poison or anything."

Mrs. Adams said, "Oh, I don't think that you will poison me. I just never saw such things and I'm wondering how they work."

"They are called aspirin and they work for any number of things." *I wish they were invented already! She could really use them for those migraines.*

Mrs. Adams placed them in her mouth and took a big drink of her lemonade. The tablets were still in her mouth after she swallowed and tasted terrible. Her face scrunched up with disgust.

"Tip your head back so they fall to the back of your throat and then swallow," Mrs. Hawk advised.

Mrs. Adams took another drink of lemonade, tipped her head back and swallowed again. This time they went down her throat. She placed the glass down on the table and stood up. "Thank you. And thank you so very much for your hospitality, your trust, and your patience with us. I just cannot thank you enough."

"Oh, now, now, dear. It is I that should be thanking you." Mrs. Hawk turned to look at Heath and Hadden and thought, *Yes, thank you for taking care of Heath and Hadden.* "All three boys are such fine young lads!"

Hadden got up off the chair. "Mrs. Hawk, can I give you a hug?"

"Oh my! Of course, dear! You don't have to ask to give me a hug. I always take 'em whenever I can get 'em." She opened her arms wide for Hadden to come in for a hug.

Hadden wrapped his arms around her. "My mom says you should always ask before you go intruding in someone's personal space. Not everyone likes a hug, believe it or not." When he let go he said, "Thank you Mrs. Hawk. I will never forget you."

"And I will never, ever forget you. I promise." She held up her right hand and winked.

Hadden smiled. He then turned around and walked towards the door. But on his way out, his arm hit one of the teacups that were sitting on the table near the door and it fell to the floor. "Oh no!" he exclaimed.

Mrs. Adams stood up as Mrs. Hawk walked over to Hadden to help pick it up. Hadden felt so bad as he looked at the V-shaped chip in the cup that tears began to form in his eyes.

Mrs. Hawk took the cup from him and placed it back on the tray with the rest of the set. She took Hadden in her arms and hugged him again. "Don't you concern yourself with this little cup. Remember, people are special, not things. So what, there's a little chip in my cup? All that means is that every time I look at it, it will always remind me of you and that's a memory that I never want to forget."

Mrs. Hawk let Hadden go and they were both smiling. "Thank you, Mrs. Hawk," Hadden said as he wiped his eyes. "I am really sorry about your teacup. Maybe someday I can come back and see you again."

"I would like that very much indeed."

"Can I tell you a secret?" Hadden asked.

"Certainly," she said as she bent over for him to reach her ear.

Instead of saying something in her ear, Hadden gave her a kiss on the cheek. "Good-bye." He turned and walked out the front door to the carriage and a waiting Mr. Belcher.

Mrs. Adams was smiling at Hadden's and Mrs. Hawk's special moment. She watched him walk down the steps then turned to Mrs. Hawk who was still smiling from ear to ear. "Thank you once again. I'm sorry for the teacup. It's a beautiful set."

"It's no big deal," Mrs. Hawk assured her. "I got that from a friend that came back from England two months ago. Before she left I mentioned to her that I heard of a new company called Aynsley that makes fine china. So while she was there she picked up this tea set for me. The flowers are called heather."

Mrs. Adams gasped. "Oh my, Hadden was saying that his name would have been Heather if he were a girl. I wondered what the flower looked like when he was telling me about it. I can see why his mom would like them." She turned to look at Johnny.

Johnny knew that was his que to say goodbye. "Good-bye, Mrs. Hawk. It was a pleasure meeting you and thank you for the cookies and lemonade. They were delicious."

"Well, I'm glad you enjoyed them. Goodbye, dear."

Mrs. Adams and Johnny turned around and started towards the carriage. Suddenly, Mrs. Adams realized that Hadden was there by himself with Mr. Belcher and they were talking. She began to panic and picked up the pace to the point where she was almost running in hopes that Mr. Chatterbox didn't spill the beans so to speak.

Puzzled, Johnny hurried along beside her. "Mama, is there a reason for the sudden speed? We just ate cookies and you always say it's not good to just eat and run."

"Yes, I have my reasons."

Heath was still standing there waiting to say goodbye. "Thank you very much, Mrs. Hawk."

Mrs. Hawk opened her arms. He went in and she hugged him tight. "I know that this has been a very scary time for you, but I want you to know how proud I am of you and your bravery. You and Hadden are very special boys and have a great destiny." Heath smiled and let go of her waist. "Now, be sure to keep that emerald in a safe place. I have a feeling that you may need it someday. Now get going before it gets too dark. Goodbye, honey. You *will* get home, I promise." She gave Heath a smile and a wink.

Heath turned around to leave but stopped in his tracks. He turned back around and asked, "Mrs. Hawk, you believed us when we said that we traveled through time without any questions, do you believe that someone can move something with just thinking about moving it?"

Mrs. Hawk's surprised expression made Heath sorry that he mentioned it. *Oh my! He does have the powers of his ancestors! He is destined to be a very great sorcerer, indeed! Yes, this task of mine cannot wait any longer,* she thought. "Oh, my dear boy, yes! I do believe in time travel, I do believe in magic, and yes, I do believe in telekinesis. Do you think that you have that power?"

Heath looked down not knowing if he should be completely honest with her but he made it this far. "Yeah, I can make things move by just thinking about it. Watch." He looked at the blanket that was hanging nicely on the back of the chair in the foyer. The blanket rose up and unfolded itself, and slowly made its way to Mrs. Hawk and wrapped around her shoulders. "Wow, I can't believe it did exactly what I wanted it to do. I did it by accident before and I've been afraid of it."

Mrs. Hawk was not surprised that Heath could do it; she was surprised by the demonstration being done so well, but the biggest surprise to her was that he was capable of doing it at such a young age. " When did you discover that you had this ability?"

"It started a few days ago. I guess on my birthday."

Telekinesis just a few days ago! And he does it like he's been doing it for years. What else has he inherited, I wonder? "Well, it seems that your birthday has been the starting point of the gift of telekinesis. That is a great gift and you must use it only for good. Have you discovered any other gifts?"

"Gifts!? How can you call it a gift? It's not a gift! It's a curse! I'm a freak of nature and no one will like me when they find out that I'm a freak. And no, I don't have any more, do you think I'll get more? Wait! Oh my gosh, today when Johnny was telling me a story about him and his mom, I pictured everything in my mind like it was my own memory. Then when Johnny stopped talking, the memory just kept going and I remembered what Mrs. Adams was wearing and what she said. I could smell houses burning, hear cannons booming and guns firing, and even men screaming. There was no other sound around except for the battle. It felt so real to me. I even told Johnny what his mom was wearing and what she said to him. He asked how I knew. I don't know, it just seems like a memory to me. It's just one that isn't mine. Yup, I'm definitely a freak of nature." Heath nodded as he confirmed his last statement.

Mrs. Hawk smiled while she held his shoulder and gave it a little reassuring squeeze. "You certainly are not a freak of nature, my dear. Every single person God created is like a diamond in their own way. Some are more polished than others only because they believe in themselves. Once you believe in yourself, you will sparkle like the diamond that you are, I can guarantee you that! Whenever you think you're alone, just remember that you just haven't met the other people like yourself. God created you with your special qualities and talents for a reason and God doesn't make mistakes. Now, let me show YOU something." She closed her eyes and the blanket that Heath had wrapped around her shoulders suddenly lifted and rose above her. It drifted over to the chair where it originally came from and slowly draped itself over the back of the chair. "I don't do it as well as you do, but I do get the job done," she said with a smile.

Heath could have been blown over with a feather. He was astonished at what he just witnessed, but it gave him great comfort knowing that he wasn't the only freak of nature in the world. "Whoa! Oh my gosh! You're a freak too!"

Mrs. Hawk laughed at Heath's enthusiasm. "Well, I have the power of telekinesis just like you do, and I can also remember everything that I ever learned. It is like a photo-graphic memory I suppose you could say, but it's not just for the things that I see, it's for the things that enter my brain. I can recall it all."

"Oh my gosh! Me too!" Heath exclaimed. He was getting more and more excited and wanted to know everything about her. "Wow, and you're so old so that means that you probably have a big brain to hold it all." After the words came out of his mouth, Heath realized that his comment could be taken as an insult. "Oh, I'm sorry, Mrs. Hawk, I didn't mean—."

"That's fine. I'm not sure if it works like that, but it seems that you and I are foxes from the same den," Mrs. Hawk said as she laughed and tousled his hair. "Now listen to me care-fully, you will discover that you will suddenly have powers to do other things as well. I don't know what they will be or when it will happen, but it won't be anything that you can't handle. God has given you your abilities for a reason. Who knows, maybe you were meant to be a hero, someone with a great destiny." She placed her hands on his shoulders. "However, for now, you must not keep Mrs. Adams and everyone waiting any longer. When we meet again, I will explain more to you but for now, you must be going and be safe," she said as she turned Heath around to face the front door and gave him a little nudge.

Heath felt such relief after talking with her and ran down the walkway to the carriage.

Marian Hawk stood on her front porch and watched them ride away. As the carriage drifted off into the distance, her heart was so full of love that it could just burst. She was beaming with so much pride and admiration for those two little boys. Not many people can say that they met their great, great, great, great, great, great, great grandsons.

★ CHAPTER TWELVE ★

MR. BELCHER WAS STANDING BESIDE THE DOOR OF THE carriage waiting as Hadden made his way down the long sidewalk. "How was your visit with Mrs. Hawk?"

Hadden took Mr. Belcher's extended hand and climbed into the coach. "It was good. I really like Mrs. Hawk. She gave me cookies and lemonade. The cookies were really good too. I never had any like that before. Then when I was leaving I accidentally knocked over a tea cup. I felt so bad because I broke it and it was a really pretty tea cup. But Mrs. Hawk didn't get mad at me. She hugged me instead. She really is a great lady."

"Yes, Mrs. Hawk is a very fine lady. I'm glad you enjoyed yourself." Mr. Belcher turned around and suddenly Mrs. Adams was standing there with rosy cheeks and a little out of breath. "Are you alright ma'am?" he asked as he held her hand to help her up into the carriage.

"Oh, I think it's just a little too hot and I walked a little too fast," she said, trying to make light of her sprint.

Johnny sat next to Mrs. Adams and gave her a curious look. "Mama, you didn't just walk a little too fast. You raced me to the carriage."

She looked at Johnny and smiled. "Yes, and I won." She took a deep breath and thought to herself that she must be getting up there in age quicker than she thought. She caught her breath and realized that her head didn't hurt anymore.

As they were waiting for Heath, Hadden leaned over and whispered, "Mrs. Adams, are you going to take us to the cave and watch us leave?"

"Of course, dear. I wouldn't let you leave all by yourselves. I want to be sure that you go safely back to your time," she said and thought that she wanted to see this for herself.

Heath joined them in the carriage with a feeling of relief and excitement.

Hadden realized that Heath took the longest of all of them leaving. "What took you so long?" he asked.

"I don't know, we just talked a little," Heath said with a smile.

Mr. Belcher made his way up to the driver's seat of the carriage to begin the long ride home.

After their time with Mrs. Hawk, the boys were very anxious to get back. Since it was summertime, it didn't get dark until about 9 pm. That gave them four hours to walk through the woods to the cave. With a full moon it wouldn't get pitch dark, but Mrs. Adams wanted to be out of the woods by the time it started to get dark. They had candles and lanterns but she'd rather not have to use them.

Johnny thought about Sophia and wondered about her. "Mrs. Hawk said that she was best friends with Sophia's mother, Daisy, and that Sophia was there just to help take care of her. Do you think Sophia is a slave, Mama?"

"No, I believe she is there taking care of a family member, Mrs. Hawk."

Johnny nodded. "Yes, I thought that too. I can't wait until slavery isn't allowed anymore."

Hadden didn't understand what they meant. "What's slavery?" he asked.

Heath gave Hadden a nudge in his side and whispered, "Shh. Not right now."

"What? Why?" Hadden had no idea why he should shush. He thought it was a simple question, especially since Johnny was the one that said the word first.

Mrs. Adams wondered if Heath felt uncomfortable talking about it with Mr. Belcher here. She leaned forward towards Hadden and whispered, "How about we talk about this later? This is a bit of a bigger conversation than just answering your question right now. Is that acceptable to you?"

At that moment, Mrs. Adams made him feel like a very

important person. He leaned in toward her and said, "Yes, it is acceptable, Mrs. Adams." Then Hadden whispered, "Can we stop somewhere and go to the bath... ah... use the... uh... na-nex-tree?" He still needed a bit more practice at the whispering part of a whisper though.

Mrs. Adams smiled because she knew Hadden was trying to say the necessary or privy. Heath heard it too and laughed so hard that his stomach muscles began to hurt. Heath's laughter was contagious and Johnny started laughing too.

Mrs. Adams looked at Heath and Johnny, wondering what they found so hysterically funny. She turned around to the front. "Mr. Belcher, I neglected to have the children use the privy before we left and now Hadden feels the need to use one. What do you think about stopping along the way for him to—" Then she realized why Heath was laughing so hard and let out a giggle herself as she said, "for him to use 'the next tree'."

"Yes, ma'am. Right up here is a good place to stop."

The carriage came to a stop and Mr. Belcher came around to open the door for them. "We still have about thirty or so minutes until we arrive at home. Why don't all of you go before we get started once again," Mrs. Adams advised.

"Well, I don't have to go right now, but I can try," Heath said.

"Yeah, Mom always says if you don't feel like you have to go right now just try," Hadden said.

Hadden realized that they had to actually go into the woods to relieve themselves as not to be seen by Mrs. Adams. "Ya know, Mr. Belcher, I think it might be a good idea if you come with me in case a bear jumps out when I'm going."

Mr. Belcher wanted to laugh but held it back. "I think that is a good idea. We don't want you tripping over your knickers and getting eaten by a bear, do we now?" he said.

Heath stood there and shook his head at Hadden. "Why do you always worry about bears? They are probably more afraid of us than we are of them."

Johnny stepped down from the carriage. "I saw a black bear two years back. They are tall and scary. I can see why Hadden would be afraid."

"You lads have nothing to worry about. I will make sure that there are no bears and if I see one, I will yell 'bear' before he has a chance to get too close," Mr. Belcher assured them.

"Sounds like a plan, my man," Hadden said as he started walking towards the woods.

When all three boys were finished, Heath held his finger up to his lips and said, "Shhh, I thought I heard something." They all stood frozen in place listening. Mr. Belcher turned around and Heath yelled, "Bear! Run!"

Johnny and Hadden screamed like little girls and went running as fast as the wings on a hummingbird. Johnny fell over the uneven ground and Hadden tripped and landed right on top of him. They heard Heath behind them laughing and Mr. Belcher ran to see if Johnny and Hadden were hurt.

Heath walked slowly towards them feeling bad about them falling down at his joke. "Are you two okay?"

Hadden was just standing up and said, "Yeah, Johnny broke my fall this time."

Johnny stood up but then he yelled, "Oooouch," and lifted his right foot. "I think I broke my leg."

Mr. Belcher was very concerned. "Don't stand on it, let me pick you up and carry you to the carriage."

Johnny waved his hand and said, "No, no, just help me walk to the carriage, please."

Mr. Belcher took hold of Johnny's arm and slowly began helping him limp to the carriage. Johnny took three steps and looked back at Heath. He looked very worried. Johnny put his foot down and said, "Ha, I got you back!"

The relief on Heath's face was instant. Heath let out a deep breath and laughed. "Ah man, that was a good one."

Heath held up his fist for a fist bump. Johnny looked at him quizzically. "You're supposed to make a fist and we bump them together. It's like a high five but with your fist."

Johnny made a fist and bumped Heath's fist. "What's a high five?"

Heath laughed and explained, "It's another way of saying I like what happened, or congratulations, or whatever.

We smack each other's hands while they are up in the air. We have five fingers so it's called a high five."

Johnny nodded and smiled.

Mrs. Adams met them at the edge of the woods. She exclaimed, "I heard screams and thought that you may have been hurt!"

"No, it was the lads just having some fun," Mr. Belcher explained.

"Yes, Heath yelled 'bear' and Hadden and I screamed. It was funny, I must say." Johnny laughed again.

Mrs. Adams let out a sigh of relief. "Well, come then, we must get back."

As Mr. Belcher helped them up into the carriage, he posed an unexpected question to Mrs. Adams. "Ma'am, I hope it's not too forward, but I just have to ask. Was Mrs. Hawk able to help with getting the lads back home to their time somehow?"

Not only was Mrs. Adams surprised that Mr. Belcher asked the question, but was surprised that he knew the reason for the visit to Mrs. Hawk's.

Mr. Belcher explained, "You see, Sophia is my cousin and her mom is my aunt. That is how I know of Mrs. Hawk and her stories. I never believed it was true until I saw Heath and Hadden. Their manner isn't like others that I know of. Hadden acted like he never saw a horse up close before, which is unusual for anyone here. I wondered about that. Then, I heard Hadden ask about slavery, and then he asked if you were going to the cave with them." Mr. Belcher looked at Hadden. "You need a little practice on those whispering skills, little man," he said with a wink. "I always thought there must be something to those stories but when Johnny came out to ask if I knew Mrs. Hawk, I thought it odd. Then when Hadden slipped while exiting the carriage, he mentioned that he would hate to break something while he was here in 1776. That confirmed my suspicions. That's when I knew they must have come from somewhere other than a different town."

Mrs. Adams felt relieved that she didn't have to keep this a secret any longer. Mr. Belcher was a free man and had been with her for a long time. She considered him a good friend. Now she wasn't completely alone in trying to help these two boys go back home. "Yes, Mrs. Hawk said that they must go to the cave that they came out of with a special emerald that they had found."

"When is it that they came from, may I ask?"

"2024." Mrs. Adams replied.

Mr. Belcher's eyes got wide. After the information sunk in, he said, "Oh, alright, let's get these lads home." He jumped up onto the driver's seat and began the ride back.

"Since all of us know where Heath and Hadden come from, I would like to take advantage of this time we have and find out what the future is like. Would you tell us..." Mrs.

Adams paused for a moment. "Oh my, there are so many questions I have that I don't know where to begin."

Johnny asked the first question. "What about slavery?"

Mrs. Adams exclaimed, "Yes! Let's begin with that. Is slavery still in existence in the year 2024? I think it's dehumanizing and I hate it immensely."

Heath said, "No, we had a President named Abraham Lincoln who freed all the slaves."

Mrs. Adams, Johnny, and Mr. Belcher cheered. They didn't know what a president was, but all they basically heard was there was no more slavery.

"But what *is* a slave?" Hadden asked.

Heath looked at Hadden and wasn't quite sure how to answer that. Mrs. Adams stepped up to the plate. "A slave is a person who is made to be someone's property and do whatever that person wants them to do. They are not treated very well either."

"Abraham Lincoln freed the slaves in 1862 with the Emancipation Proclamation and on January 1, 1863, all the slaves were free. But since word traveled so slowly back then, well, like here where there are no phones and television to tell the world all at once, word finally got to the last state of Texas about the Proclamation on June 19, 1863. Our president now made June 19 a federal holiday and it's called Juneteenth," Heath explained.

Hadden was shocked that a human being would think it's alright to own another human being. He didn't learn that in school and wondered how Heath knew it. "How do you know all this stuff?"

"Don't you remember last summer when we went to the Smithsonian Museums in Washington, D.C.? We learned about all kinds of things. I wanted to go to all of them but we only had a week and didn't have time. Dad said we could go back this year and he said the best part is that it is ALL FREE. There is no charge to get in!"

"Well, it must have been boring and I wasn't paying attention."

"Probably," Heath agreed.

"Slaves are freed in 1862? I wish I could see the day when that happens," Mr. Belcher said as he cheered again.

"Yes, I do too," Mrs. Adams said as she turned to Heath. "Can you tell me about the women?"

Heath didn't completely understand the question so he just looked at her with a blank look on his face.

"How are the women treated? Can they go to school?" Mrs. Adams was so passionate about women's rights that she enthusiastically began preaching. "I believe that women should not be content with the simple role of being companions to their husbands. They should educate themselves and thus be recognized for their intellectual capabilities, so they can guide and influence others. Just a few months back, I wrote just that statement to Mr. Adams. I told him that I am hoping that he directs congress to remember the ladies, and be more generous and favorable to them than their ancestors and not put such unlimited power into the hands of the husbands. If particular care and attention is not paid to the ladies we are determined to foment a Rebellion, and will not hold ourselves bound by any laws in which we have no voice, or representation." She stopped speaking and realized she was sitting straight up waving her fist in the air and most likely, scaring the children. "I do apologize. I care very much about this issue. Not so much for me, but for Nabby and posterity. So, my question is, are women treated better in 2024?"

Johnny always knew that his mother believed in women's rights but he had never seen her talk about it with such passion. He just sat there looking at her in astonishment.

Heath too was taken aback by her outburst to answer right away, but he did understand how it was important for women to have rights. He had learned about how they weren't allowed to vote for a president until 1920. He remembered it specifically because he thought of his mom not being able to vote when his teacher said that Black men were granted the vote in 1870 but it took another fifty years for the women to get that right.

Since Heath wasn't answering her, Hadden took advantage of the moment to ask, "Who's posterity?"

Mrs. Adams looked at him and smiled. "Posterity means future generations."

Heath was finally over the shock of Mrs. Adams' outburst. "Yes, women pretty much have equal rights. They can vote for a president and do anything they want. Right now our Vice President is a lady named Kamala Harris. She's the first female to hold the office in the history of America. My mom says 'Just wait, it won't be long before there is a woman president!' And you know what else? There was already an African American president named Barack Obama!"

Mrs. Adams, Mr. Belcher, and Johnny were speechless as their brains processed this information then Johnny sat forward and asked, "Can you explain what a president and vice president is? I'm not sure I understand."

Hadden jumped in to try and explain. "The president is the person that runs our country and the vice president helps. Sorta like Batman and Robin."

Heath laughed out loud, Mrs. Adams and Mr. Belcher looked confused at the explanation.

"What's Batman and Robin?" Johnny asked.

Heath answered. "Batman is the one in charge and Robin is his sidekick."

Johnny looked excited and said, "Oh, it's like the Generals and Commanders!"

"Okay, I guess," Heath said and laughed.

"So who will be the first president of our country?" Mrs. Adams asked.

Hadden jumped at the chance to answer the question. "The first president was George Washington!"

Mrs. Adams practically choked at the news. "General George Washington is the very first president!?"

"Yes," Hadden said.

Mrs. Adams was shocked at first, then the excitement started forming. She just couldn't believe all this information. She was excited that women and negroes would be able to do anything, even become president of our new free country. She was so happy she wanted to jump around and dance. Mrs. Adams enthusiastically asked, "You mentioned that America has a national anthem. Now that we have the time, would you sing it for us?"

Heath looked at Hadden and asked, "Do you know all the words to the Star-Spangled Banner?"

"No, do you?"

"Yes, but most of the time it's only the first part sung. How about if we sing the first part of the song together for them?"

Mrs. Adams said, "How many parts are there to this song?"

"There's about four parts to it, but most of the time the first part is only the part that is sung."

"I'd love to hear any part of it that you know," Mrs. Adams said.

"Okay." Heath said. As he cleared his throat to get ready to sing, Hadden began singing. "O beautiful for spacious skies..."

"That's not the Star Spangled Banner, you goofball. That's America the Beautiful," Heath interrupted.

"Oh, how does the Star Spangled Banner begin?" Hadden asked.

"It starts with Oh, say can you see..."

Mrs. Adams interrupted them, "There's a song called America the Beautiful? I would love to hear that one as well."

Hadden said, "Okay. We'll start with America the Beautiful and then we'll sing the Star Spangled Banner. Okay?"

"Okay. On three. One, two, three." Heath instructed.

Heath and Hadden began singing, "O beautiful for spacious skies, for amber waves of grain, for purple mountains majesties, above the fruited plain! America! America! God shed His grace on thee and crown thy good with brotherhood, from sea to shining sea!" Hadden let his voice go higher and drag the word out longer as he sang the word sea.

While he was singing, Heath noticed a low lying branch sticking out that was going to hit the carriage as they passed. He remembered Mrs. Hawk said that he has a gift that he should use for good so he thought about it breaking off the tree and by the time they passed, the branch was on the ground.

Mrs. Adams, Johnny, and Mr. Belcher applauded when they were through singing. Mrs. Adams said, "I think it's wonderful that America and our flag have their own songs. What a great country America becomes!" Mrs. Adams was tearing with pride and happiness that America will become such a great nation that songs are dedicated to it and the people are proud to be American. Johnny and Mr. Belcher sat back with deep reverence. Since no one was saying anything, Hadden said, "Now let's do the Star Spangled Banner for 'em."

"Sure," Heath cleared his throat and nudged Hadden to sing with him."Remember, it starts with 'Oh, say, can you see'?" Heath reminded him then began singing. Hadden joined in a second later.

"Oh, say, can you see? By the dawn's early light

What so proudly we hailed at the twilight's last gleaming;

Whose broad stripes and bright stars, through the perilous fight,

O'er the ramparts we watched were so gallantly streaming.

And the rocket's red glare, the bombs bursting in air.

Gave proof through the night that our flag was still there:

Oh, say, does that star-spangled banner yet wave?

O'er the land of the free and the home of the brave!"

All three of them applauded. Mr. Belcher even had a glimmer of a tear in his eye but Mrs. Adams was almost bawling. She reached inside her dress and took out a piece of cloth and wiped her eyes and nose with it. "This gives me so much hope for America's future."

"Where did this song come from? I got chills down my back!" Johnny said with emotion.

Hadden said, "I know this one! Frankie wrote it!"

Heath palmed his forehead and shook his head at Hadden. "Where do you come up with this stuff?" Everyone laughed at Heath's reaction.

Hadden explained, "When we were in the Smithsonian looking at the flag that inspired the song, Dad said that the song was written by Francis Scott Key and his nickname was probably Frank 'cause Dad's uncle had the same name. Then I said, 'Then his name is Frank Key,' get it? Frankie." Hadden laughed.

"Only you could come up with something like that," Heath said, shaking his head. "Actually, at the Smithsonian, I learned that in 1814, 'Frankie' got the idea to write a poem about what he saw during the War of 1812. He was supposed to help make an agreement between the British and the American forces for the swap of a prisoner during the Battle of Baltimore."

"Now hold your horses there, Einstein," Hadden interjected. "You just said that it was in 1814, during the War of 1812, and then you said the Battle of Baltimore. I don't think you know what you're talking about."

"Yes I do. Just listen slowly and then you'll understand."

Heath explained, "I asked Mom about it and she said 'A war is like a big, long lasting thing that can last years. The battles are the fights during that war. Like the Battle of Monmouth that was in our town during the Revolutionary War.' So that means during the War of 1812, which started in 1812 in case you couldn't figure that out," Heath said sarcastically, "and ended a few years later. The Battle of Baltimore was fought in 1814. Don't you remember this from the Smithsonian?"

"That's probably when I had to go to the bathroom so Dad took me and we got lost. So we just kept looking around while you and Mom looked around somewhere else."

"Oh" Heath shrugged. "That makes sense."

"You have mentioned this Smithsonian quite a few times, what exactly is the Smithsonian?" Johnny asked.

"It's actually called the Smithsonian Institution in Washington, DC, and it's a world-renowned museum and research center that has about 20 museums, galleries, and even a zoo!"

Johnny noticed that they only had about ten more minutes together in the carriage. "Heath, please go on with the story. I'm afraid I won't be able to hear the entire thing because we are almost home."

"Well, Frances Scott Key, or Frankie," Heath laughed, "was sent to help make an agreement to swap prisoners, but since he was on a British ship and he overheard the plan to bomb Fort McHenry in Baltimore, the captain was like, no way you're leaving now to go warn everyone of our plans. The captain said that they wouldn't shoot the bombs off if the fort lowered their American flag. The Americans said nah-uh and refused and Frank was stuck there while the British ships bombed Fort McHenry and couldn't do anything about it. Then night time came, whenever a rocket went flying off in the air, it had this red glare that gave off enough light to see our flag was still flying high and proud. Then there was so much smoke with all the firing that he couldn't see anything anymore. He had to wait until the sun rose in the morning to see anything. When it did, our flag was there still waving! And that's the flag that I saw in the Smithsonian, it's colossal!" Heath said as he held his arms out for effect.

Mrs. Adams was so moved that she still had tears in her eyes. "Heath, you really know how to tell the story. No wonder Frank Key was inspired to write about it. America is something special to fight for and from what you told me, it gives me more passion to see it free from British rule."

Heath smiled. "It will be. Someday America will have presidents instead of kings and queens."

★ CHAPTER THIRTEEN ★

Satan came running from around the back of the house. He ran up to Johnny wagging his tail joyfully. He acted like he hadn't seen him in over a week when it was only a couple of hours. Johnny squatted to pet him. "Holla, boy. Were you a good boy while I was gone? Oh, of course you were!"

Hadden didn't forget what Mrs. Adams had said before they left. "Can I go help with the horses now?"

"May I help too?" Johnny asked.

Mrs. Adams asked Mr. Belcher, "How long does it take to undress the horses?"

"Not very long."

Mrs. Adams thought for a moment what she had to do. "Well, I think we will have enough time for everything here, then to go through the woods to take Heath and Hadden to the cave and then back again before darkness sets in, don't you?"

"Yes, I think we have plenty of time, ma'am."

"I'd rather not be roaming around the woods in the dark, but just in case, let's not forget the lantern."

"I will make sure we have one, ma'am."

The boys got back inside the carriage to ride around back to the barn. Mr. Belcher turned around to Mrs. Adams. "When we finish up with the horses, I will send the boys back to the house."

"That sounds fine, thank you. I must go see how Mary and Nabby are doing with the boys. You know how rambunctious they can be when they are getting hungry." Mrs. Adams turned around and walked towards the house.

Mr. Belcher drove the boys around to the barn while Satan ran behind the carriage. When the horses were stopped in front of the barn, Mr. Belcher went around and helped the boys get out of the carriage. Hadden was so excited to help with the horses. He couldn't believe how tall they really were when you stood next to one. "Do horses ever bite people? You never hear them biting people. I watch a lot of movies and TV shows and the horses on there never bite the people. I saw a show where the kid gave the horse a carrot? Do they like carrots? I bet they do since they showed it on TV. Do they eat other vegetables too? I don't like vegetables, Mom puts cheese on them like they are gonna taste better or something, but they still taste just like vegetables but with cheese on 'em."

Heath rolled his eyes. "Okay, Sir Talks-A-Lot, give it a rest."

Mr. Belcher laughed.

The horses were standing in front of the barn ready to be untacked. "Now, since you have never been around horses, the first thing I want you to know is that you don't want to stand behind a horse. I learned the hard way. I have the scars to prove it," Mr. Belcher informed them.

"What happened, Mr. Belcher?" Johnny asked.

"When I was a young lad I wasn't paying attention while my daddy was untacking the horse. I stood behind it and for some reason the horse kicked me. The tip of the hoof got me right on the back of my shoulder." He tapped the spot on his shoulder where the horse had kicked him. "Now, you boys stand over there in front of the barn while I unstrap the belly strap and, hmm..." He thought about everything that had to be undone and decided it would just be faster if he didn't explain everything. He should find something else for them to help with. "How about if I untack the horse while you keep him busy while I do that? How's that sound?"

All three boys said in unison "Sure."

Johnny quickly said, "Jinx," and all the boys laughed. Mr. Belcher looked at them and shook his head and smiled.

Mr. Belcher went inside the barn to retrieve two little buckets of apples and one little bucket of carrots and gave each boy a bucket.

Mr. Belcher showed them how to give the horse an apple.

He held out his hand face up and palm flat and placed the apple on his palm. The horse took it gently out of the palm of his hand. "Now, if you do it just like that, your fingers won't get in the way when he grabs the apple. Do you think you can do it like that?"

The boys stepped up to feed the horses the first of many hand-fed apples.

Mr. Belcher said, "I've seen people get their fingers bitten and then blame the horse like it was the horse's fault. Usually when an animal bites you, or does anything wrong, it was because of something that the person did wrong with the animal."

Mr. Belcher looked at Heath. "Why don't you give Caesar a carrot?"

"What's the name of this horse?" Hadden asked as he pointed to the other white horse.

"This beauty here is Cleopatra. Caesar and Cleopatra are Mr. Adams' favorites and he's had many horses. He certainly finds the best names for his pets, doesn't he?"

Hadden said, "Hi Caesar." He looked up at Mr. Belcher and asked, "Can I pet him?"

"Sure, go ahead, he loves people. That is why he is bringing his head down. For you to do just that."

Hadden was fascinated by the size of everything about this wonderful animal. "Wow, their nose is really, really big!"

Heath laughed. "Of course it is, ya dork. Look at the

size of 'em. You would have to have a big nose with a body this big."

"Yeah, you're right, for once." Hadden laughed and tapped him on the shoulder with the back of his hand. Then he added, "Can you imagine the boogies that come out of that nose?" making everyone laugh.

Mr. Belcher finished untacking the horses and brought all the equipment into the barn and put it away. "Now we just have to bring them into the barn and brush them down." He turned to Johnny. "Johnny, do you know how to walk them?"

"I saw you do it hundreds of times, I think I can do it."

"I think you can too," Mr. Belcher said encouragingly. They walked both horses into the barn and Mr. Belcher hooked Caesar's lead onto a hook. Johnny was a little too short to reach so he waited for Mr. Belcher to hook Cleopatra's.

"I am going to get the brushes and show you how to brush them," Mr. Belcher said as he walked away. He came back and demonstrated how to brush the horses on the sides but he had to do the backs of them since the boys couldn't reach.

"Okay, now we just have to feed them their hay and give them water. Johnny, how about you go with Heath and fill the water buckets and Hadden will help me get the hay."

Johnny grabbed the buckets and handed one to Heath. As they walked out of the barn, Heath thought about what

Mrs. Hawk had said about his gifts. "Hey, Johnny, do you believe that people can move things with just their mind?"

Johnny lifted an eyebrow as he had never heard of such a thing. After giving it some thought, he furrowed his eyebrows and said, "Well, if I hadn't met you today and someone asked me that, I would say no, however, after meeting someone from the future, I can believe anything now. So my answer to your questions is yes. Is moving things with your mind something common for everyone in the future?"

"No, it's not. Before I left Mrs. Hawk's, I asked her about it and she said that it's a gift and that I may get more gifts and that I should only use them for good."

They reached the well and Heath dropped his bucket on the ground while Johnny went to tie the bucket onto the rope. While Johnny fiddled with the rope he accidentally dropped it into the well. "Oh goodness!" he said as he was looking down the well. "There goes another bucket!" Johnny turned to Heath and said, "I have dropped so many buckets down there that I am most sure that there must be over a hundred buckets down there."

Heath and Johnny looked over the side of the well and Heath could see a glimpse of the bucket before it went completely under the water. He closed his eyes and thought really hard about the bucket. Suddenly it rose upside down and continued rising up until Heath grabbed it and tried handing it to a very astonished and speechless Johnny.

"Oh, I should have turned it the other way so it would have been full when it came up, that was silly on my part." Heath smirked. "I will bring the other buckets up that you say you lost too." He turned around, closed his eyes and imagined buckets like the one he just had in his hand sitting on the bottom of the well. Suddenly he could hear the splash of water spilling out of the buckets as a half dozen of them rose up from the bottom of the well. He had them rise up over the wall of the well and gently placed them on the ground next to it. "There, that should do it."

If a strong wind blew, it could have knocked Johnny over. He stood there like a statue in complete silence.

"Are you okay, Johnny?" Heath asked.

Johnny took a moment and then slowly nodded.

"I just started being able to do that the other day," Heath admitted.

Johnny's shock wore off, "Oh my! The things that I could do with a gift like that!" Johnny exclaimed. "I could do chores while I am sitting under a tree making things happen with just thinking about it. That would be wonderful!"

Heath didn't think of that before! He couldn't help but smile at Johnny's excitement. "Huh, that's a great idea! Ooh, but Mrs. Hawk said that I should only use my ability for doing good. I don't think that would be a good deed," Heath said with a laugh.

"Would you empty the buckets back into the well? I'd like

to see more of this great talent of yours?" Johnny asked.

"Sure," Heath answered as he thought of lifting the buckets up. All except one bucket rose while splashing water here and there. They moved over the side of the well and tipped, allowing all the water in them to fall back into the well. When they were empty, he lowered them down to the ground. "There, how's that?"

"Oh my heavens! I can see that being a gift. Not only can other people not do that, but imagine the things that you could do with it!" Johnny exclaimed.

"Well, I have to get used to this. I'm afraid to let other people know that I can do it because they will think I'm a freak. I told you because you're not from my time and I trust you."

"Thank you for trusting me with your secret, my friend. I will never tell anyone, I promise," Johnny said as he raised his right hand.

"I guess we should head back now. They may be wondering what happened to us by now," Heath stated as he lifted one of the buckets.

Hadden tagged along after Mr. Belcher down the center of the barn to where the hay and grain were kept. Mr. Belcher took some hay out of a bale and said, "Here, you take this for Ceasar and I will take some for Cleopatra. Then we will have to get some grain for them because they will need more than just the hay."

"Okie dokie, Mr. Belcher. Thanks for letting me help. This is a lot of fun."

Mr. Belcher smiled. "This is a great help to me. Thank you." He scooped the grain out of a barrel and poured it into a bucket. "Now, can you do that for your bucket?"

"I sure can!" Hadden exclaimed. He took two scoops out and poured it into a bucket, then carried the bucket over to Cleopatra's stall and placed it on a hook on the wall just as Mr. Belcher placed his bucket of grain in Caesar's stall.

Cleopatra came over to him and Hadden slid his hand down her nose a few times. "I really like horses. Do you ride on them sometimes, you know, on top of them?"

"Yes, sometimes we do when we need to go somewhere."

"You don't ever ride for fun?"

Mr. Belcher laughed. "No. When you do something all the time, it isn't as much fun anymore as it was the first time."

Hadden thought of that for a moment. "Yeah, you're right. I remember when I was real little I wanted to go to school like Heath did, but then when I had to do it every day, I didn't want to anymore."

"What do you do for fun in the year 2024?" Mr. Belcher asked.

"Well, we do all sorts of stuff. We go to museums, base-ball games, the beach, amusement parks. Oh, and you know what? Last year we went to Washington D.C to the Smith-sonian and New York and saw The Statue of Liberty. She stands in the New York Harbor on Liberty Island holding a torch. She was a gift to America from France and is a Roman liberty goddess wearing a robe. It's pretty cool. She has her right foot raised showing that she is walking forward with a broken shackle and chain." Suddenly the light went off in Hadden's head, "Ooh, now I get it! Liberty means free and the shackle and chain shows that she broke free. Huh, sometimes things just sink in later when you think about it again. Right, Mr. Belcher?"

Hadden didn't wait for an answer, "Ooh, and we went to the new One World Trade Center building. I had to say the new one because the buildings that were there before came down on September 11, 2001, by terrorists that crashed planes full of people into it and the buildings came down. That was the worst day America ever saw, but One World Trade Center is the tallest building in the United States! Mr. Belcher, that's humongous! It is 1,776 feet tall! They did that on purpose to symbolize the signing of the Declaration of Independence! They also call it the Freedom Tower because of that."

Heath and Johnny came walking in with the buckets of water. "That was something else! It's a lot of work to just get some water." Heath and Johnny smiled at each other.

Hadden looked over and said excitedly "Yeah, isn't that cool?"

"Yeah, but I wouldn't want to do that all the time though," Heath stated.

Mr. Belcher was still in shock over hearing Hadden say that there was a building 1,776 feet tall. He just couldn't imagine such a thing.

Johnny looked at Mr. Belcher. "What do we do with these now?" he asked as he picked up his bucket a little higher.

Mr. Belcher shook his head to come back to reality. "Uh, you can hang a bucket of water next to the feed buckets on the wall in each stall." Heath went to Caesar's stall and Johnny went over to Cleopatra's stall and placed the buckets on the hooks. "Good, now let's close the stall door so they can eat. We must get going to get you two boys to the cave." Heath stayed a minute longer petting Caesar's nose. "He really likes you. You seem to have a way with him. He gives me a hard time sometimes."

"I like him too." Heath finished petting Caesar, then turned around, walked out of the stall and closed the door. "Are they gonna stay in there now for the night?"

"No, when I come back, I will send them out into the fields for them to run around and play."

Hadden was amazed. "Horses play?"

"Sure, all animals love to play. All animals have feelings and emotions. They can be jealous, empathic, happy, sad, joyous, they love, and even mourn when a loved one dies. Not a lot of people know that about animals. That's why we should treat all of God's creatures with respect and love." Mr. Belcher paused for a moment. The boys knew by the look on his face that they were about to hear a story and anxiously waited. "Actually, last month a couple of lads came across a swan's nest with a couple of eggs in it. These hell born babes thought it fun to break her eggs. Well, swans mate for life. The male swan left her because of the stress of it and the female died two weeks later of a broken heart. I believe all God's creatures are equal to ourselves because God created them just as much as He created us. We must treat ALL living things with respect and love."

Heath nodded in agreement. "My mom says God created all things for a reason, even bugs have their reasons so I don't even squoosh bugs!"

"Yeah, and I know animals love and all the other feelings you mentioned. I know my dog loves me," Hadden said with a smile. "He follows me everywhere." He leaned in to get a little closer to Mr. Belcher and whispered, "I think Zeus loves me more than Heath."

Johnny laughed. "Satan loves me more when Papa isn't around. When he is, then Satan is always by his side."

Hadden still needed to practice on that whispering. Heath heard what he said to Mr. Belcher and retorted, "Nuh-uh, Zeus follows you around because you always have a snack in your pocket."

Hadden stuck his tongue out at Heath who, in turn, had to stick his tongue out at Hadden.

Mr. Belcher smiled. "I bet your dog loves both of you just

the same. Let me ask you something as we get going." He turned to Hadden. "You said the building you saw was 1,776 feet high to symbolize the signing of the Declaration of Independence. Does that mean we become free from British rule *this* year?"

"Yes," was all Hadden said.

"Were you telling Mr. Belcher about the Freedom Tower?"

"Yeah, and the Statue of Liberty."

While they were having this conversation, all four of them began walking out of the barn. Heath thought how excited Johnny and Mr. Belcher were about America's independence that maybe they might be happy to learn about the Constitution and the Bill of Rights. "My teacher said things were still hairy when the country was formed. The states and Continental Congress weren't playing nice and thirteen years later they had to create something that splits the government up in three different parts so one of 'em isn't more powerful than the other, like a king. So they made the Constitution. It splits the states and the government up and we elect the people that work there. The Constitution became the Supreme Law of the United States. Then they did the Bill of Rights for each individual."

Johnny asked, "What is a bill of rights?"

"It's THE Bill of Rights. It's ten things the government has to make sure that they give to people. I only know the first three, but there's ten of 'em. The first one is freedom of speech, religion, and the press; the second is the right to bear arms; the third is the government isn't allowed to have troops live in your house and eat your food." Heath had a look of realization at that moment. "I think that came from this time period. The British are taking over any house that they want to and kicking out the people that live there or making the people make food for them and everything. Aren't they, Mr. Belcher?"

"Yes, they are." Mr. Belcher was surprised before but now he was flabbergasted at all this news.

Johnny was just as surprised and wanted to know, "So the Supreme Law, the Constitution, is written thirteen years from now so that means that it is written in 1789."

Heath said, "Well they started writing the laws in 1787 but it took a couple of years to take effect."

Johnny thought about this a moment longer. He found it very hard to imagine that laws that would be written in 1789 would still apply to the generation of 2024. "So, these laws are written in 1789, and you say that it will *still* be the law of America in 2024? The laws of the Colonists never changed in over 200 years?"

"Oh heck yeah, they changed a lot! The way that the Constitution was written allowed for changes. They are called amendments. The first ten are the Bill of Rights. Another one got rid of slavery. There were twenty-seven amendments made so far. One of them was that no one was allowed to drink alcohol and then another one took that amendment away and made it okay again. Isn't that funny?"

Johnny and Mr. Belcher were silent as they absorbed all of this information. All four of them were all walking side by side with Hadden on the right end of the line next to Heath. Hadden looked over down the line, then he looked straight ahead, straightened his back, pushed his shoulders back, and began walking with a strut.

Heath looked over at him. "What the heck are you doing?"

"I'm pretending we're in a movie and we're all walking down the road being cool."

Heath laughed out loud and said, "You're such a dork."

⋆ CHAPTER FOURTEEN ⋆

MRS. **A**DAMS WAS TAKING OFF HER APRON AS THE BOYS walked into the kitchen. "Heath, Hadden, it's now half past seven and we haven't a lot of time to take you and come back before dark, so I am afraid that there isn't time for us to sit and have dinner together, as much as I would have loved to do just that. We must get going. You don't know if we may run into trouble or not."

"Okay, Mrs. Adams, we are ready to go, beli-eeeeve me," Hadden said as he nodded his head for emphasis.

Heath nudged Hadden. "Cut it out, nimrod."

"No, you cut it out," Hadden said while backhanding him in the chest.

"No, you," Heath said while backhanding him back.

Mrs. Adams rolled her eyes. "Boys, that's enough. Go up stairs and get your clothes and make sure that you have everything—especially that emerald."

Heath and Hadden said in unison, "Okay."

As they turned to run to the stairs, Heath quickly tapped Hadden on the arm and said, "Jinx."

"Wait for me," Johnny yelled to them. "I would like to go upstairs with you, if you don't mind."

Hadden said, "Dude, it's your house, why would we mind?" which made everyone smile.

On the way up, Johnny said, "You know, ever since you came here, I have felt like I have made very good friends and I hate to see you leave. I wish there were a way to write to you."

"Yeah, that would be really cool. I feel like I have made a good friend too," Hadden said.

Heath agreed. "Yeah, I feel the same, Johnny. In our time we have things like the computer and cell phones that we can talk to people all the time wherever they are. I wish you had one too so we could talk to you too."

"I just can't imagine all the things that you speak of."

"Yeah, now that I have some understanding of how things are in your period of time, I can see why," Heath said with a smile.

In the bedchamber, Hadden grabbed his shorts and flung them over his arm, causing something to fall out of his pocket. Two pieces of gum and a Pokemon fell on the floor. All three boys glanced down and saw the little blue toy. Hadden bent over to pick it up. "Oops. Glad it's not the emerald."

"May I have a look at what fell out of your knickers?" Johnny asked.

"Sure," Hadden said as he handed the toy to Johnny. "This is a toy called Squirtle. He's from a game we have where there's a bunch of monsters that have special powers and Squirtle has the power to squirt water from his mouth real hard. They come from the world of Pokemon and we collect them too." As he was explaining he handed Heath a piece of gum. "Do you want to try chewing a piece of gum? You just put it in your mouth and chew on it."

"Oh, yes please!" Johnny took a piece and as he unwrapped the gum he asked, "So you just place it in your mouth and chew. What is the purpose of it?"

Heath and Hadden couldn't help but laugh.

Heath, still laughing, shrugged. "Because it tastes good."

Johnny placed the Bubble Yum piece in his mouth, chewed a few times, and began smiling. "This is marvelous!" Trying to talk with a piece of gum in his mouth for the first time made a little drool escape his lips. He wiped it off with the back of his hand. "It tastes like." He paused and thought about what it tasted like.

Heath asked, "Does it remind you of any fruit?"

Johnny thought hard as he chewed. It was getting easier to talk in between chews. "I have never tasted a fruit that tastes like this. What is it supposed to taste like?"

"It's strawberry flavored," Heath answered.

Johnny was surprised. "I have never had a strawberry

that tasted like this. What is it made out of? When are you supposed to swallow it?" he questioned.

"You're not supposed to swallow it. When you're finished with it, you throw it away." Hadden explained.

"Throw it away? Where?" Johnny asked.

"You throw it away in the trash." Hadden replied.

Heath realized that in Colonial America, things probably weren't thrown away like they are in 2024. "All the stuff that we don't want anymore we throw into a can. Then a big truck comes and takes it away."

Johnny wasn't truly understanding it all but caught what the idea was about. "We throw unwanted items into the privy. I am guessing that is where this gum goes when finished?"

"Sounds about right," Hadden said with a laugh.

"I don't know what it's made out of but we like it. Watch this." Heath stuck out his tongue, stretching the gum, and blew a bubble.

"Oh my heavens!" Johnny exclaimed. "How did that happen? Will you show me how to do the magic also?"

The boys laughed at Johnny's reaction and Heath explained how to spread the gum over your tongue, seal the opening between the gum and your lips, and then blow. Johnny tried a few times and on the fourth try made a little bubble. He took it out of his mouth and studied it then put it back into his mouth. From his reaction, you would have thought that he just made a home run with two outs and the bases loaded.

"That's awesome Johnny!" Hadden exclaimed.

The boys spent another five minutes blowing bubbles then Johnny finally asked, "May I take it out now?"

Heath said, "Yes, whenever you want."

Hadden explained. "I always put mine back into the wrapper. Once I learned that birds look at it and think it's bread and die from it, I ALWAYS throw it away in the trash."

Johnny remembered the toy he had in his hand and began studying Squirtle. He was fascinated with the material it was made out of, the color, the texture, the smell, and the shape. "Humph, it is an interesting little thing," Johnny said with a smile.

Before Johnny could ask any questions about this amazing thing he was holding, Hadden said, "Keep it, Johnny. This way you always have something to remember us by."

"Oh, I certainly don't need something to remember you by, but I will cherish it to say the least. Thank you."

"You're welcome," Hadden said with a smile.

"Wait, I want to give you both something to always remember me by." Johnny looked over in the corner and picked something up. It was a circular disk with two holes in the center, like a button, with a string in each hole and the ends were tied together. It was small, easy to use, and easy to carry. "Here, I would like to give you my whirligig to remember me by," he said as he looked at Heath. "This is how you play with it." Johnny held the ends of both strings while the disk sat in the center. He spun one hand around, making the string get taut, then pulled them apart. The disk whirled and buzzed around while the string twisted forward and backward.

Johnny handed it to Heath and he tried it for himself. "That's pretty neat. Thank you, Johnny."

"You're welcome, my friend. I hope it always reminds you of me whenever you play with it."

Johnny gave Hadden a little wooden stick with a cup on the top and a ball attached to a string. "This is a game called ball and cup. You try to catch the ball in the cup. It sounds rather easy, but it is challenging. Both of these games are very popular."

Hadden looked at it and noticed that it had the initials JQA on the bottom of the cup. "You put your initials on your things too? Heath does that too. He says I take his stuff all the time."

"You do, ya little dipsy doodle."

Hadden ignored Heath's comment and tried his new toy, "Wow, this is a challenge. Thank you, my friend."

As Heath and Hadden gathered up their belongings, Heath turned around to look at Johnny. "You want to know something?"

"Yes."

"Whenever I think of today I will always remember what you and your mom did for us. Thank you for helping us."

"We didn't help you yet, you're still here," Johnny said with a smile.

"No, I mean taking us from the woods to your house and believing us. I don't know if anybody else would've believed me. I don't think that I would have if I was in your shoes."

"Yes, I do know what you mean. When you first told me your story, I thought maybe the heat got to you or something. You may even have been thought of as a lunatic or a spy." All three boys laughed.

Hadden started taking off his shirt and Heath asked, "Should we change into our clothes now or later?"

"No, Mama said to get your clothes, not change them."

"Ah, okay."

Johnny thought about that for a moment. "Maybe she's afraid someone will see you before we get to the cave."

Hadden said, "Well, that makes sense," as he put the shirt back in place. He looked at Heath and asked "Are you ready to go?"

"Yeah, do you have the emerald?"

Hadden stuck his hand in the front pocket of his shorts and pulled it out. "Yep, it's right here."

"Okie dokie dude, let's do it," Heath said as he walked out the door.

As they made their way downstairs to the kitchen Hadden felt a ping of hunger and said, "Boy. I'm starting to get hungry. I hope we get home soon so we can eat supper, oh wait, dinner," and laughed to himself.

Heath smiled at Hadden's comment then noticed Mrs. Adams standing in the kitchen by the back door. Mr. Belcher, Nabby, Tommy, and Charlie were there and Mrs. Adams was telling Nabby something about what to do while she was gone. It appeared that Nabby would be babysitting Tommy and Charlie once again while Mrs. Adams, Mr. Belcher, and Johnny walked with the boys to the cave.

Mr. Belcher could hear the tension in Mrs. Adams' voice. He knew she wasn't afraid of walking through the woods in the dark. She was the toughest woman he'd ever met. Well, after his own Mama, that is. He figured she must be worried about whether the boys would be able to get home.

Mrs. Adams turned around towards them and said, "Alright, I think that we are ready to go now. Do you boys have everything that you were wearing when you first came here?"

Both of them nodded and Heath said, "Yes, ma'am."

Mrs. Adams looked at Hadden. "Do you have the emerald?"

"Yup, right here." He lifted his shorts up and patted the pocket.

Mrs. Adams asked, "May I see this emerald, if you don't mind?"

Hadden took the emerald out of his pocket and handed it to Mrs. Adams. She held it up at eye level. "Oh my, it truly is beautiful." She squeezed it in the palm of her hand to see how it felt and if it got warm. "It's not getting warm."

"Maybe it only works when you're in the cave," Mr. Belcher suggested.

Mrs. Adams explained, "Mrs. Hawk said that it has something to do with the bloodline. Apparently the boys are from that bloodline. I, however, am not." She handed the emerald back to Hadden. "Here you go, make sure you put it back in your pocket so you don't lose it."

"'Kay."

They exited the house through the back door. Satan came running up to Johnny, hoping for some fun. Johnny squatted down to Satan's level to pat him on the head. "Come on, boy, we have to take a walk through the woods."

Since it was after seven, it was getting a little cooler. Not much, but you could feel the difference. Mr. Belcher grabbed the lantern just in case they didn't make it back before it got dark. He walked in step with Mrs. Adams. Johnny, Heath and Hadden all went ahead of them but leading the way was Satan, who had to sniff every branch, tree, and blade of grass there was along the way.

Mrs. Adams said to Mr. Belcher, "I am concerned for the safety of these two boys. I have grown quite fond of them. If they do go through a, dern, what did Mrs. Hawk call it now?

Hmmm. A different dimension, I think, how will we know if they made it back to their time period?"

"I had the same worry. Then I thought if these two lads are here, they must be here for a reason that is far beyond our understanding. I will have to leave my faith in the Lord that He will take care of them."

"Oh, I know you are right on that but it doesn't make it any easier." She sighed.

Johnny and the boys were walking single file down the path in the woods after Satan. Hadden was bringing up the rear of the three. Johnny turned around. "So you never told me what you do for fun in your time period."

Heath said, "Well, you already know we have baseball, but we also have football which is played with a ball that's kinda oval."

"What do you do in a game that requires an oval ball?"

"Well, wow, it's hard to explain the whole thing in like five minutes."

Hadden said, "No it's not. There are two teams and eleven people on each team. The field is one hundred twenty yards with field goals shaped like this on the ends." Hadden held out his arms and folded his arms up at his elbows trying to imitate a field goal post. "The ball is in the center of the field and the way you win the game is trying to get the ball down to the end of the field to the goal line." He looked at Heath and said, "See, it wasn't that hard Mr. Smarty Pants."

Heath turned around and stuck out his tongue at Hadden.

Suddenly Satan took off through the brush. Johnny yelled, "Satan, come back!"

Mr. Belcher was much taller and could see a bit further out over the brush. "It's okay, Johnny," he said. "Satan is trying to catch a rabbit. He will be right back because you know he never catches one."

Johnny felt relieved and laughed.

"Ooh dat wascally wabbit," Hadden said, trying to imitate Elmer Fudd from the Bugs Bunny cartoons. He and Heath were the only two that saw the humor in it.

Satan came rushing back and took the lead again. About thirty feet ahead, Satan took a left turn at a stone wall that began right where the path ended. Johnny said, "I know you have to go this way," and pointed to the right. He gave a whistle for Satan to follow and a few seconds later Satan was in the lead again.

Hadden said, "Oh yeah, we also play board games and video games. Video games are on TV, a computer, or some screen or another. Mom won't let us play anything that is killing people or anything rough like that. Right now I'm in the middle of playing *Marvel Super Heroes*. I have to try to save earth from the bad guys. I like Spider-Man the best because he can shoot webs from his hands. He has spider-senses to spot objects that others can't see and he can crawl up walls. Heath just got a new game for his birthday last..."

"Okay, Sir Talks-A-Lot. Give it a rest," Heath interrupted.

"Oh zip it, Mr. Smarty Pants."

Johnny smiled. "I actually enjoy it. With times so stressful right now in the middle of this war, anything that takes our minds away for a bit is always welcomed." A minute later, suddenly Johnny said, "I think the cave is right up this way. Satan was just there a moment ago but then just disappeared. I am guessing he ran into the cave."

Hadden said, "Well, I hope he wasn't eaten by a bear."

Heath rolled his eyes and held up his hands when he said, "Oh my gosh, what is it with you and..."

Johnny interrupted before Heath could finish his sentence. "Yes, here it is!"

Mr. Belcher and Mrs. Adams caught up with the boys in front of the cave. "Come on, it's this way," Hadden said as he waved them in. It was a little dark but their eyes adjusted fast.

"Now, according to Mrs. Hawk, you just have to place the emerald in the palm of your hand. It should get warm and that's when you will be able to just go through the cave wall, but make sure you hold each other's hands. This way one of you isn't left here." Mrs. Adams raised her eyebrows and said, "I really can't believe I just said that, but life is full of mysteries that even we are not capable of understanding."

Hadden took the stone out of his shorts pocket. Mrs. Adams said, "Perhaps you should change into your other clothes before you go. You don't know where you will end up.

You don't want to be wearing those clothes and stand out in your own time."

"Ooo yeah. Thanks," Heath said.

Hadden was trying to undo the button of the knickers when Heath said to everyone, but especially to Mrs. Adams, "Um, would you mind turning around while I change?"

"Oh my, of course not! I apologize." Mrs. Adams, Mr. Belcher, and Johnny turned around. All of a sudden Satan came running out from the back end of the tunnel of the cave. He was covered in powdery dirt but was happy to be exploring all over. Apparently he had checked everything there was to see because he went out into the woods looking for something else to do.

While Heath was tying his sneaker he looked over to his brother. Hadden was on the ground flipping his sock under his toes. "Doofus, we don't have all day! Why are you worrying about lumps in your socks now?"

"Cause I can't walk with lumps in my socks. How many times are you gonna ask me that to get the same answer?"

Heath rolled his eyes and shook his head while he handed the clothes back to Johnny. "Thank you," he said.

"Yeah, here's mine too, thanks."

Johnny took the clothes from the boys and placed them on a rock that was there. "You're welcome."

Mrs. Adams was getting more scared and even emotional. She was not the kind of woman that gets emotional, either. "Even though we have only known each other for a day, you will forever be in my thoughts. You have given me hope for our future and helped me do something that I haven't done in such a very long time -- you made me laugh. You also made me believe in something as far-fetched as time travel!" She laughed. "Thank you." She then held their heads in her hands while she gave them each a kiss on the forehead.

Mr. Belcher said, "It's been a pleasure for me as well. Thank you boys, and safe travels."

"Yes, everything Mama said is true for me as well. I will miss you, friend," Johnny stated.

Hadden looked at Mrs. Adams. "Mrs. Adams, can I give you a hug?"

She smiled. "Yes, of course you can!"

Hadden gave her a hug and then Heath followed suit and said, "I want to thank you for helping us. I don't know what we would have done without you."

"I think you both are very strong, intelligent boys and would have done just fine. But I am glad Johnny found you first." She smiled.

Hadden went over to Mr. Belcher and hugged him without even asking. Mr. Belcher was a little taken aback by it but was grateful for it. Then Heath hugged him too.

Last but not least was saying goodbye to Johnny. Hadden was going to hold his hand out to shake it because he thought it would be cooler. Johnny just grabbed him and gave him a hug. Hadden couldn't help but smile. "For a kid from 1776, you're a pretty cool dude. I will never forget you for as long as I live. I will never forget any of you," he said as he looked at Mrs. Adams and Mr. Belcher, which made them both smile.

Johnny smiled. "I will never forget you either." He was going to miss his newfound friends from another time period.

Mrs. Adams asked, "Hadden, where is the emerald?" Hadden took it out of his pocket and showed her. "Alright, remember just wrap it in your palm, like you did before." Hadden began wrapping his fist around it to show her how he did it.

While he was hugging Johnny, Heath said with a sad little smile, "I will never forget you, Johnny. Hadden is right, you are a pretty cool dude."

As they let go of each other Johnny said, "I will never forget you either." He flashed a devilish little smile and added, "Ya dork."

Mrs. Adams' eyes almost popped out of her head and her hand went up to her chest as she exclaimed, "John Quincy! You mind your manners, young man!"

Johnny didn't care. Heath and Johnny kept grinning at each other. Heath thought to himself, *His middle name is Quincy, that's a pretty cool name.* Then he said his entire name in his head: *John Quincy Adams.*

He froze and a chill went down his spine. His eyes got wide, his jaw dropped, and he couldn't speak or move. In his mind he was replaying the entire day ever since he got here.

The entire time Heath was having this realization, the stone was beginning to tingle in Hadden's hand and it started to give off some type of illumination. Hadden exclaimed, "Oh my gosh! It does glow! Alright, Heath, let's go."

Heath was still in stunned silence. Mrs. Adams didn't know what happened to Heath but was worried that there may be a short period of time for them to go when the emerald started to glow. "Hadden, hold his hand and just pull him through with you. Just make sure that you don't let go."

Hadden took Heath's hand but then thought *I'm not taking any chances, we're going out the way we came in.* Then he wrapped his arms around his big brother and pulled him towards the wall of the cave. He had just enough strength to jump backwards to hit the wall while holding Heath in his arms. Then they vanished.

★ CHAPTER FIFTEEN ★

HADDEN AND HEATH FELT THE SAME STRANGE SENSATION that they felt when they went through the wall of the cave before. They landed in a heap on the cave floor. Hadden was too afraid to open his eyes right away. Finally after ten seconds he opened them but couldn't see anything except the back of Heath's head.

Suddenly they were being licked to death by a dog. Hadden was so upset thinking that it was Satan licking him that he wanted to cry. Heath finally rolled off of him and Hadden sat up and saw that it was Zeus! Zeus was so excited to see his boys that he was whimpering and began jumping on them with excitement.

"Zeus! Buddy! We made it back! We made it back!" Hadden shouted with excitement as he hugged him tight. When he looked at Heath, he was just sitting there, still shocked by the entire experience. Hadden asked, "Are you okay? What happened? You froze like someone hit you with a magic wand and turned you to ice."

Heath began speaking in a loud whisper, as if he were talking to himself. "The entire time we were there, we were hanging out with John. Quincy. Adams. The sixth President of the United States of America! I never thought that John Quincy Adams was once a nine-year-old kid." Then his voice began growing louder with excitement. "His father is John Adams! The first Vice President of the United States AND the second President of the United States! He is a founding father of America AND is even considered to be the 'father of the Navy'! He was in Pennsylvania all that time creating the Declaration of Independence while we were there. I thought Johnny's father was just in some other town doing lawyer stuff. I didn't think about any-one's names while we were there. I was just worried about getting home."

"And we made it home!" Hadden said enthusiastically.

That's when Heath snapped out of the shock and looked around. "Oh my gosh! We're back home!" Heath shouted. Oh my gosh! Just wait until Mom hears about all of this!"

"Look, doofus, let's think about this. Do you think Mom is going to believe us? We are going to go home and she is going to ask us how our day was and you are going to tell her that you found a time traveling stone and we went to

1776 and hung out with John Quincy Adams and his family. Think about it for a minute."

Heath stood there considering the possibilities. "Well, if we tell her the truth, she will think that we were just making it all up. Plus the fact that she will probably think we are losing our marbles. Shoot, I don't think we can tell anyone about this. How would anyone believe us? Wait! Mrs. Adams believed us."

"Yeah, but we looked like a couple of loony birds with the weird clothes and sneakers. And we didn't talk like them and, well, I dunno, Mrs. Adams is just more, ah, open minded to something like time travel I guess. Do you think Mom would be?"

Heath thought for a moment. "No, I don't think she would be. So I guess we can't tell anyone. This just has to be our thing."

"Ab-so-freakin-lutely!"

Heath asked, "I wonder if it's still the same day here as it was when we left?"

"Well, Zeus is still here so it has to be the same day."

"Not really, he could have gone for a while and just happened to come back and we popped in."

"Well, I guess we won't know until we leave, so let's go," Hadden suggested.

They began walking out of the cave. Heath stopped at the entrance of the cave to look around and see if anything looked familiar. He thought it did. He made a right out of the cave, the opposite way in which they came there originally.

Hadden said, "Zeus, take us home, boy!" Zeus looked at him with his tongue hanging out of his mouth, his ears perked up and was ready to go. He began leading the way, about twenty feet ahead of them.

They made it to the edge of the woods and saw the lake and their fishing poles and tackle box still there leaning against the tree where they left them. The boys had never felt so relieved in their short lives. Hadden looked across the lake and noticed the same people that had been there before. "Heath! Look, it's the same people! It must be the same day!"

Heath was so excited that he made a fist and brought it down as he said, "Yes!"

"Do you know what?" Hadden asked. "I don't care if you know or not, I'm gonna tell ya anyway. When I was little and still in kiddygarden, Mom forgot to pick me up from school. Remember that? You took the bus all the time but Mom had to get me. I was so scared that I was never gonna see her again. I thought I was gonna have to go home with Miss Kemper and live with her forever. Then when Mom came in the door, I was so happy to see her. I think seeing this lake makes me even happier than that day."

Heath nodded and said, "I know what you mean, blue jean."

Hadden grabbed the tackle box and started walking beside Heath who was holding the fishing poles.

Heath said, "Man, I still can't believe today happened. We became friends with the sixth president of the United States of America! Man oh man."

Hadden nodded his acknowledgment. "Ya know what I'm thinking? I don't think we should give this emerald to Mom. I'm thinking that we should use it again. Whoa! Wouldn't it be cool if we went to the time of Jesse James and became part of his gang or back to when the dinosaurs roamed. Holy fudge muffins! That would be awesome!"

Heath laughed, "Eh, I dunno about going back to the dinosaurs, but I think it would be cool if we went into the future though. Yeah, we shouldn't give it to Mom. We should try it out again. Man, I still can't believe today happened. It's like a dream."

Hadden kicked a stone and nodded. "Yeah. I'm still kinda freaked out about it though."

Heath was still wrapped up in his thoughts to have truly absorbed what Hadden had just said. "You know, I know some of who the presidents were but I don't know a lot about most of them. Like with Washington, everyone knows that he was the first president. Oh man! When they asked who the first president was I should have told them that John Adams was the first vice president. Then we would have found out who they were before we left. Darn."

Hadden agreed, "Yeah." That was all he was able to get out when Heath cut him off.

"I guess living in Freehold made it more interesting to me so I remember a lot about Washington. Washington led the troops in the Battle of Monmouth on June 28, 1778. It was the longest battle of the Revolutionary War. He was fighting the British that were led by General Henry Clinton. My class walked down Main Street to Clinton's Headquarters too. Actually, General Charles Lee..." Heath's eyes grew bigger. "Oh my gosh! Johnny told us the story of General Lee and his dog, Spada, and I didn't even think about who he was talking about at the time. I was just so scared."

Hadden was listening intently then asked, "Yeah, I was pretty scared too. What happened to General Lee?"

"Well, Washington really wanted to attack the British but he was too far away with the rest of his troops so he sent General Lee and some men to just to like, tease the British to keep them around until Washinton got there to whoop their butts. Lee had no idea that Washington had his men trained to fight during the winter in Valley Forge because Lee was held captive for 16 months by the British. So when the British turned around and started coming towards Lee and his men, Lee chickened out and retreated. They ran into Washington and the rest of the troops that were coming. Boy, was Washington mad. The fighting stopped when it got dark or somethin' and when the morning came, the British were gone.

Chickens! And I remember the story of Molly Pitcher during the Battle of Monmouth too. She was one of the women that brought water over to the men while they were fighting 'cause it was so hot and humid that day people were dying just from the heat. Her nickname was Molly and the men would yell 'Molly! Pitcher!' and that's where the name Molly Pitcher came from. It turned into a nickname for the women that brought water to the men. And you know what else?" Heath didn't give Hadden a chance to answer. "That water wasn't just to drink either. The guys at the cannon had to use it to soak sponges to clean out gunpowder and make sure all the sparks were out of the barrel of the cannon after each shot."

Hadden was impressed that his big brother knew all this. "How the heck do you know and remember all this stuff?"

Heath thought about Mrs. Hawk and smiled. "I don't know." They walked quietly for a moment when Heath stopped walking, turned to Hadden and asked, "Ya wanna know something, Hadden?"

Hadden got a worried look on his face since Heath called him his given name. That meant something serious was about to happen. "Yeah, what."

"We have to keep this time travel a secret and I trust you to do that. I also trust you to keep a secret that I pretty much got around my birthday. Okay?"

Hadden nodded and anxiously waited to hear this big secret.

"Since Mrs. Hawk believed us about time travel, I thought I'd tell her my secret. When I want to move something, I just think about it and it happens. Mrs. Hawk said I have telekinesis. She believed me without even questioning me about it and then she told me that she has it too! Then she told me that she remembers everything that enters her mind, just like me! She said they were gifts. Oh, and a weird thing that kinda freaked me out was having someone else's memory in my head like it was mine."

Hadden was rightfully shocked by Heath's secret. He began thinking that his big brother has lost his mind. It must be from the flip of going to 1776. Finally he blurted out, "Okay, show me, magic man."

"Okay, look over there at the gnome in Tommy's yard under that little tree," Heath said and proceeded to raise the gnome up off the ground, let it hover for a second, turned it around and placed it back down facing the house. "I'll make that leaf over there on the ground come to me." Heath stared at the leaf and suddenly it rose up and floated to Heath, where he snatched it from the air.

Something magical happened at that moment: Hadden was completely speechless.

"Mrs. Hawk said that it's a gift, but I don't know what I'm supposed to do with it. If it's a gift, it should be something good, right?" Heath questioned but didn't wait for a response. "What good can you do with something like this?"

Heath looked at Hadden and waited for an answer, but Hadden was still at a loss for words. "Wait, before I left Mrs. Hawk's she said when we meet again she'll explain more to me. Does that mean that we will go back to 1776 again? Does it mean that she will come here to 2024? I wonder what she meant? Aren't you going to say anything?" Hadden looked at him and shook his head. "I don't know much about Johnny but now I'll have to go home and find out more about John Quincy Adams."

They were so engrossed in their thoughts that they passed people at the lake without even realizing that they were even there. Zeus was always just ahead of them sniffing in the grass, on the trees, in the bushes, anywhere he could. His boys were back and all was right in the world again. He stopped for a moment to look at a girl screaming in the lake. He had to be sure that she didn't need help and when he saw that she was just screaming from having too much fun, he continued his job of sniffing some more.

Hadden's mind was cluttered with so much shocking information today that he couldn't sort it out enough to even think clearly about any of it. They traveled back through time, hung out with a president while he was still a kid, and then he found out that Heath had this special power of moving things with his mind. Hadden decided that he was going to give his head a break and not think about any of it any more right then or his head might explode. He'd had enough crazy for one day. "So what are we gonna tell Mom that we did today?" Hadden finally asked.

"I dunno, just let me do all the talking though, okay?"

"Yeah, Okay. You say that now but I bet when the time comes, I'm the one that winds up saying something first because you freeze under pressure."

Heath looked at Hadden and said, "No I don't. Okay, I'll make you a bet, you take out the trash for a week if I don't do all the talking and if I do, then you name it."

"Deal," Hadden said.

When they made it out of the woods, there wasn't anyone around. They expected to see people out in their yards or kids playing. They walked down three houses and on the side of the third house a man was lying next to a motorcycle. He had tools and a rag in his hand. He saw the boys and waved. Heath and Hadden waved back and Hadden said, "If Mr. Stephens is outside working on his bike, that means it's about seven o'clock. He does that after he gets out of work while Mrs. Stephens makes dinner."

"How the heck do you know that?"

"'Cause I talk to him all the time."

"Do you know everyone in the neighborhood, for Pete's sake?"

"Well, yeah, I get around, big brother, I get around," he said with a slight smile. "I always ride my bike down here to Brian's house. I like talking to the people along the way."

Heath smirked. "Well, that is something that you're very good at."

Zeus was sitting at the corner waiting for the boys to come and tell him when to cross the street. Heath looked both ways and said, "Cross." All three walked across the street. "I bet everyone is in their backyards or eating dinner. That's why there isn't a lot going on around here."

Hadden agreed and said, "Yeah, could be, or it's just too hot. I know I'm starving."

They continued in silence just thinking about the incredible day that they had and Heath's secret.

Along the way they saw Mr. and Mrs. Lopez sitting on their front porch. Mrs. Lopez waved to them and said, "So, how'd you do?" Heath and Hadden looked strangely at Mrs. Lopez because they had no idea what she was talking about. "Did you catch anything?"

Hadden realized she saw the fishing poles and shook his head. "Oh, nope, we didn't."

"Oh well, maybe you'll have better luck next time. You should try going early in the morning when it's not so hot," Mr. Lopez advised.

Heath said, "Yeah, this weekend we are going to go with my dad. Have a good night, Mr. and Mrs. Lopez."

Mr. and Mrs. Lopez both waved and said, "You too!"

The boys made it to the Petersons' house and Zeus was already sitting next to Danny on the front step enjoying all the pets he was getting. Danny said, "Hey, what are you guys doing? Wanna hang out and jump on my trampoline?"

"Nah, maybe tomorrow. We have to go home and eat and stuff," Heath replied.

Heath and Hadden walked over to the side of the bushes. Both of them peeked around the bush to see if Mom was around. Zeus went running to the back yard in search of a ball.

"What are you doing?" Danny wanted to know.

Hadden turned around and looked at Danny. "Nothing."

"We're pretending to be spies and we have to sneak around so no one notices us," Heath remarked.

Danny got excited about being a spy and said, "Ohh, can I play?"

Heath answered, "We have to go home for dinner now but we can tomorrow though."

"Okay! I'll see you tomorrow." Danny sounded really excited.

Heath noticed his dad's car was in the driveway but his mom's was gone. "Guess what? Mom's not home, let's go."

They ran over to the side of the house and ducked down so they couldn't be seen from the windows once again.

Heath stopped and peeked around the corner of the house to make sure his dad wasn't sitting there. Then he ran across the backyard to the garage door and opened it quickly. Hadden took off quickly and tripped. The tackle box fell to the ground. Lucky for them it stayed intact but made a lot of noise.

While Hadden was getting up off the ground, Logan opened the back door. "Hey, you alright kiddo?"

"Yeah, I think that I scratched my knee on the cement, but I'll live."

Logan laughed. "Well, that's good to hear. What are you doing with the tackle box?"

Heath came out of the garage just in time to hear his dad's question and froze.

"Nothing. I was just looking in it making sure we don't need anything," Hadden explained. "I'm gonna catch Old Lucky this weekend when we go fishing. Are we still going fishing, Dad?"

"Of course, I'm looking forward to it. Now, go put that away, Mom will be home shortly. She had to run over to Mrs. McCue's to help her with something and she will be back soon and we'll eat. Mom's stopping at Federici's on her way home."

"Good, I'm starving!" Hadden felt his stomach rumble just thinking about pizza. Then he thought of Mrs. Adams' beef stew. He would never be able to have beef stew again without remembering her.

Heath rolled his eyes at Hadden when their dad went back into the house and whispered, "That was a close one."

"Yeah, if it was any closer, I'd have to change my underwear." Hadden placed the tackle box in its rightful place in the garage and they walked into the house.

"You guys should wash up and get ready, Mom called and said she's on her way home," Logan said.

Heath went running upstairs.

Hadden had placed his hand on the banister and one foot on the step. He paused for a moment and asked Logan, "Hey Dad, do you know why eggs have to be put in the fridge? Why can't we just leave 'em out on the table in a basket?"

Logan paused the TV and said, "Well, that's a strange question that just came out of the blue. What made you think of that?"

Hadden shrugged and said, "I dunno, I was just thinking about it I guess."

"Well, eggs are washed before they are placed in the cartons that we buy at the store. When they are washed, it removes the outer cuticle of the egg which protects it from germs getting into the shell. Since the shell has pores that salmonella can get into, we have to keep them in the refrigerator so the bacteria can't grow," Logan explained.

"So, if the eggs didn't get washed, we wouldn't have to put 'em in the fridge?" questioned Hadden.

"No, we wouldn't have to, but we would have to be sure to wash our hands very well after handling any eggs so we don't get salmonella. That's the reason they are washed first, but then you have to be sure to refrigerate them and cook them well."

"Oh, okay," Hadden said and headed upstairs. He wondered if Mrs. Adams knew about salmonella.

Heath was sitting on his bed looking through his tablet.

"Whatcha doin', info cruisin'?" Hadden asked.

"Yeah, I'm looking up Johnny and getting more information about him."

Logan yelled from downstairs, "You two better be washing your hands and getting ready for dinner, Mom is just pulling up."

Hailey was just walking in the back door when the boys got down to the kitchen. "Well, there you two are. What the heck have you been doing with yourselves all day?"

Hadden didn't say a word because Heath had said that he was going to do all the talking. After a moment Hadden answered his mom's question. "Eh, nothing much. Do you want me to set the table, Mom? I'm a starrrvin Marrrvin." He looked at Heath and wondered what he was going to make him do for the bet he just won.

"Well, that would be nice. Heath, why don't you get the glasses, and Hadden, you get the napkins and paper plates. So, did you both have a good day?"

"Yeah," Heath replied.

Hailey lifted one eyebrow, turned her head slightly and asked, "You didn't go fishing, did you?"

They both raised their right hands and said in unison, "Nope, we didn't go fishing. I promise."

Hadden backhanded Heath as he said, "Jinx."

★

THE END

⋆ EPILOGUE ⋆

In 2024

AFTER DINNER, LOGAN AND HAILEY WERE SITTING IN the living room talking over coffee when Logan realized that they hadn't heard a peep from the boys in quite some time. He whispered, "It's pretty quiet, what do you think our off-spring are doing?"

"I don't know, maybe we better go see."

They both quietly walked up the stairs and tiptoed to the boys' bedroom. They stopped right before the door and peeked around the corner. What they saw just made Hailey's heart melt and Logan smile from ear to ear.

Heath was sitting on the floor next to his bed with his tablet on his lap. Hadden was sitting right next to him looking over at what was on the screen. Hailey and Logan caught Heath saying, "You know what else I found out? It says that the Revolutionary War ended in 1783. It lasted eight whole years! Wow! That's a looooong time."

"Yeah, wow! That's how old I was last year!" Hadden exclaimed.

"Hey! I didn't know this! It says here that Johnny also became a leading force for the promotion of science. In 1829, British scientist James Smithson died and his will stated that his money be used to make the Smithsonian Institution an establishment for the increase and diffusion of knowledge."

"Wait, what does that mean?"

"I know increase means more, but I dunno what diffusion of knowledge is."

Hadden said, "Oh okay. You may continue now," as he waved his hand for Heath to proceed.

"In Smithson's will, he stated that his estate will go to Washington should his nephew, Henry James Hungerford, die without hairs."

"Whaaat? Hairs? You mean he can't be bald?"

"Well, I think it says hairs, I dunno how else to say this, do you —H-E-I-R-S?"

Hadden shook his head. "Nope."

"Maybe it's spelled wrong here. Well, if Smithson was into science, maybe he was trying to create a hair lotion for bald guys and if his nephew didn't have any hair when he died, then he gets zilch. I guess hair was a big thing back then."

Hadden smiled and commented, "It's a good thing it's not now. Did you ever see the back of Dad's head?"

Hearing this, Hailey had to tiptoe away a bit so her laughter wouldn't give her spying away. Logan had a concerned look on his face as he felt the back of his head, which made Hailey laugh even more, which brought tears to her eyes and even more laughter.

Heath continued reading his tablet. "Anyway, where was I? Oh, right here. The increase and diffusion of knowledge among men."

"You can stop reading now, it's boring me. Just fill me in after you get the gist of it all."

"Okay, give me a minute." Heath continued reading in silence while Hadden got up off the floor and walked over to the window to look outside. "Oh my gosh! Get this!" Heath exclaimed. "It says that there was a whole bunch of money left and the government invested it in unstable bonds, whatever that is, and they lost it fast. Johnny became the biggest supporter of the Smithsonian Institution! He fought Congress to get the funds back with all the interest and have it used for an institution of science and learning just like James Smithson wanted, for people to continue learning and share their knowledge with others." He looked at Hadden and said, "Oh my gosh! I bet that's because of us!"

Hadden's face lit up and exclaimed, "Yeah, I bet it is! It's a good thing Smithson's nephew was bald!"

Logan and Hailey had to walk away before they laughed out loud. Logan shook his head and looked at Hailey with a smirk and said, "Kids. Where do they come up with this stuff?"

Hailey nodded and laughed then said "I know, right. And I think they are calling John Quincy Adams Johnny, how cute is that? C'mon, let's go downstairs and finish our coffee before it gets too cold."

"Yeah, I'll be right down, I'm going to go to the bathroom for a minute. Honey, where do you keep the hand held mirror?" Logan smiled as he was still feeling the back of his head. "I'm just curious."

In 1776

After Marian Hawk watched her descendants ride away, she went up into her attic. The old cedar chest was dusty and hadn't been opened in a very long time. She knelt down and wiped off the dust. She unlocked it and when it was opened, the first thing she saw was a little coin purse. She opened the purse and let the five coins roll out onto her palm. She looked at the shiny bright penny, nickel, dime, quarter, and half dollar. She thought, *I can't believe these old Semiquincentennial coins that I got in 2026 feel like I got them so long ago.* In 2026 a new penny, nickel, dime, quarter, and half dollar minted for the 250th celebration of the signing of the Declaration of Independence. *And right now the reason for them hasn't even been declared yet.* Mrs. Hawk shook her head in amazement.

She put the coins back after reminiscing about them and then grabbed the old pictures in the chest. She smiled every time she looked through them. She shuffled through the photos smiling at every one of them. When she came across the one with Hailey, Logan, Heath, Hadden, and their dog smiling in front of a Christmas tree, her smile got even wider. It was taken five years ago but when she saw them today, she recognized them immediately. She couldn't help but think, *It's amazing how fast they grew up!*

She skimmed through the other pictures for a few minutes and placed them on the floor. She looked into the chest and there it was, the reason she came up here. She picked up the leather bound book and rubbed her hand across the cover and thought, *I can finally add something new to the family journal after all these years. My 7th great grandsons came to visit me with the help of the emerald from Georg's staff. I knew it was somewhere in that cave!*

She placed the journal on the floor and picked up Georg Pawer's wooden staff out of the chest. It had a figure of a dragon on top with a tongue that slithered out and the tip of it was forked. There were two holes where the eyes should be and a hole in the middle just above the eyes. The wings and tail were raised up as if it should be holding something in between them. Since a sorcerer created it, Marian thought it might be missing a crystal ball.

As she studied the staff, she was still trying to figure out what was missing in it. *Maybe the emerald the boys have goes under the dragon's right palm.* The chest of the dragon was lined with several rectangle topaz pieces except for one missing in the middle of the chest. *Obviously, it's missing a rectangle topaz and it's missing one of the rubies for the eye.* She placed the ruby pendant that was around her neck in between her forefinger and thumb and twirled it as she thought. *I have one starburst ruby for the dragon's left eye that takes me to the future. So I know I have to find the other starburst ruby that matches this one. I imagine it will take me back to the past, and there must be something that sits in the middle of its forehead.*

Marian's thoughts went back to Heath and the powers that he was gaining. *Both of them will most likely be extremely powerful sorcerers coming from such a bloodline. Heath has already gained the powers of a photographic memory, telekinesis, and surprisingly, memory walking. I wonder what else he will inherit and when it will take hold. I hope above all hope, that they inherit their sorcerer powers from Robert Howard and nothing evil from Georg Pawer. How anyone could think that they could take over an entire planet is not only crazy but evil. And to place*

Bob and his family in a spell of eternal sleep for trying to stop him is just cruel. And look what happened! Georg's spell was so powerful that it sent Theia spiraling towards earth. When it hit, it collided at a 45 degree angle and threw debris that eventually joined together to form the moon. I have heard so many stories, but I know in my heart that by having one descendant of Georg's and one of Robert's get together to form a child, that child can break the spell and finally release Robert and those of his family that were placed under the spell.

She was so lost in her thoughts that subconsciously she heard her name being called and by the third time, she realized it was Sophia calling to her to announce that dinner was being served. Marian yelled downstairs from the attic, "I'm in the attic, Soph, I will be down in a few minutes. Thank you, dear."

Hmm, I wish I could go into the future and find out what happens but every time I go to the future, I just can't find anything out, she thought as she smacked her leg with her fist. *Yes, it's now imperative that I work on this with more fervor.* She grabbed the book and placed everything back into the chest, locked it back up, and walked away to begin the most important work of her life—saving her ancestors' souls.

AUTHOR'S NOTE

You're probably aware that the Adams family was a truly iconic American family. I wanted to stay faithful to their story, so everything – from Abigail chatting with General Lee's dog to John defending those involved in the Boston Massacre – is based on fact. Even down to their pets' names! The following are a few more interesting details about the Adams family that you might enjoy.

While Georg Pawer, Audie L. Murphy, and Robert L. Howard are indeed historical figures, in my story, they are ancestors for Heath and Hadden that will have major roles in the coming books. I've taken some creative liberties with their roles, but below you'll find information about their remarkable real-life accomplishments.

As a child growing up in Freehold, New Jersey, I was oblivious to the historical tapestry woven into the very fabric of my hometown. Established in 1693, Freehold held centuries of stories within its streets and buildings. Yet, as a child, these tales held little significance for me.

Today, I feel a deep sense of gratitude for my roots in this small town with a big history. If you ever have the opportunity to visit Freehold, I encourage you to explore some of its remarkable historical and interesting sites. I have included just some of them in the following pages.

It's been an absolute pleasure sharing Heath and Hadden's journey through Colonial America with you. Their adventure was a joy to write, and I can't wait to share their next adventure to the 1800s with you. Until then, remember that what you see on the outside of a person doesn't necessarily mean that is what is on the inside. Always be kind, everyone you meet is fighting a battle you know nothing about.

INTERESTING FACTS AND TIDBITS

John Adams, Jr.

30 October 1735 – 04 July 1826

John Adams by Jane Stuart, C. 1800, Courtesy of the Adams National Historical Park Service.

One of the founding fathers of America and considered to be the "Father of the Navy." Adams fought for the establishment and strengthening of the American Navy throughout his career.

He and Abigail had six children but only four lived to adulthood: Abigail Amelia, John Quincy, Charles, and Thomas Boylston. Susanna was born in 1768 and lived to be one year old and Elizabeth was stillborn in 1777.

He was the first vice president of the United States that served under the first president, George Washington, and he was the second president. He rode to his inauguration as President in an elegant carriage pulled by Caesar and his favorite horse, Cleopatra. John Adams and his wife Abigail were the first presidential couple to reside in the White House.

In a letter dated 26 April 1777, John wrote to Abigail: "Posterity! You will never know how much it cost the present generation to preserve your Freedom! I hope you make good use of it! If you do not, I shall repent in Heaven, that I ever took half the Pains to preserve it."

The intertwined lives of John Adams and Thomas Jefferson found a poignant conclusion on July 4th, 1826 - the 50th anniversary of the Declaration they both helped shape. Adams, unaware that Jefferson had already passed that morning, uttered his final words, "Thomas Jefferson survives," a testament to their complex bond of friendship and rivalry.

Abigail Smith Adams
(Mrs. Adams)

22 November 1744 – 28 October 1818

John's frequent absences placed the burden of managing their farm and finances squarely on Abigail's shoulders. Her capable stewardship prevented financial

Abigail Adams by Benjamin Blyth, Courtesy of the Adams National Historical Park Service.

ruin, a fate that befell many other farms during that era. Abigail was far more than just John's wife; she was a true partner in every sense. As the second First Lady, she was sometimes referred to as "Mrs. President," a testament to her influence and strength.

A unique distinction is shared by Abigail and Barbara Bush: both were wives of one U.S. President and mothers to another.

A letter Abigail wrote to John on February 13, 1797, reveals her progressive views on race and education. She describes how she assisted a free Black youth who sought her help in learning to write. Despite facing criticism from a neighbor for enrolling the boy in school, Abigail defended her actions, emphasizing his right to education and self-sufficiency. Her willingness to personally tutor him in her parlor further underscores her commitment to equality, a remarkable stance for the time.

Abigail and John Adams were staunch opponents of slavery, recognizing its inherent evil and the threat it posed to the ideals of American democracy. In a letter to John on September 22, 1774, Abigail expressed her deep concern about the hypocrisy of fighting for their own freedom from Britain while denying the same liberty to enslaved people.

On March 31, 1776, Abigail expressed skepticism towards the Virginians' proclaimed "passion for Liberty", pointing out the hypocrisy of denying freedom to enslaved people. In the same letter, she also advocated for women's rights, urging John and the Continental Congress to "remember the ladies" when crafting the new nation's laws.

The over 1,200 letters exchanged between Abigail and John reveal a deep bond of love and mutual respect. Their correspondence paints a vivid portrait of their partnership, solidifying their status as America's original power couple.

Abigail Adams Smith
(Nabby)
4 July 1765 – 15 August 1813

In 1786, she married William Stephens Smith, and together they had four children. At the age of forty-six, she was diagnosed with breast cancer and underwent a

Abigail (Nabby) Adams Smith by Mather Brown, 1786, Courtesy of the Adams National Historical Park Service.

mastectomy, a procedure performed without anesthesia at that time. Unfortunately, the cancer was not fully eradicated, and two years later, after enduring significant suffering, she passed away from the disease.

John Quincy Adams
(Johnny)
11 July 1767 – 23 February 1848

John Quincy Adams, the sixth U.S. President (1825-1829), chose to be sworn in on a book of constitutional law rather than the customary Bible. Despite his Christian faith, he saw this as upholding the

Engraving of Young John Quincy, 1783, The National Portrait Gallery, Smithsonian Institution CCO.

Constitution's separation of church and state.

He was the first president to have his photograph taken.

John Adams marked a shift in presidential fashion. He was the first to be inaugurated in pants instead of the traditional knee breeches, opting for a simple, black suit made from homespun fabric. He also embraced the trend of ditching the powdered wig. These changes, though subtle, reflected a broader societal shift towards more comfortable and practical styles.

He played a crucial role in foreign policy, serving as a diplomat on the American team that negotiated the peace treaty to conclude

John Quincy Adams after Copley, 1796, Courtesy of the Adams National Historical Park Service.

John Quincy Adams, Copy of 1843 daguerreotype by Philip Haas.

the War of 1812. (A diplomat is a representative of their country who travels abroad to promote their nation's interests. They work to build and sustain positive relationships with foreign governments and foster mutual understanding through the exchange of information.)

The Smithsonian Institution ~ Despite never visiting America, James Smithson left a remarkable legacy to the nation. He died in 1829 and was buried in Genoa, Italy. His will stipulated that if his nephew died without heirs, his fortune would go to the U.S. to establish an institution for the advancement of knowledge. In 1835 his nephew died and his estate then went to America. John Quincy Adams did indeed fight to have Smithson's dream fulfilled when Congress had other plans for the money. In 1905, when the cemetery where Smithson was interred faced relocation, Alexander Graham Bell personally oversaw the exhumation of his remains, ensuring their safe transport to America. Smithson was finally laid to rest at the Smithsonian Institution, a fitting tribute to the man whose generosity made it possible.

Adams negotiated the Adams–Onís Treaty, which helped America make Florida a state.

Gag rules were essentially censorship tactics used to silence discussions on topics that the majority in power found uncomfortable or disagreeable. The most notorious gag rules from 1836 to 1844 were those related to slavery, which John Quincy Adams successfully fought to repeal in 1844. He argued these rules infringed upon the constitutional right to petition and the First Amendment guarantees of free speech and the right to seek redress from the government.

In 1841, John Quincy Adams, though serving in the

House of Representatives, took on a remarkable legal case. He defended a group of Africans who had been illegally kidnapped from Sierra Leone, sold into slavery in Cuba, and then revolted aboard the ship Amistad. Adams' impassioned arguments, delivered over two days, successfully convinced the court that these individuals were not criminals but victims of a heinous crime. The Africans were freed and ultimately returned to their homeland.

Historians agree that John Quincy was one of the greatest diplomats and secretaries of state in American history, but he was an average president. He didn't have a political personality.

In November 1846, at the age of 78, John Quincy Adams experienced a stroke that resulted in partial paralysis. Remarkably, he made a complete recovery and resumed his Congressional duties on February 13, 1847.

He chose to name his eldest son George Washington Adams, a decision that didn't sit well with his parents, John and Abigail. His second son was named John, after his own father. (It's unlikely he intentionally named his sons after the first two presidents in that order.)

John Quincy Adams also penned the Monroe Doctrine, a cornerstone of American foreign policy. This pivotal document outlined the U.S. stance on European involvement in the Americas, declaring that:

1. The U.S. would remain neutral in European conflicts and internal affairs.

2. Existing European colonies in the Western Hemisphere would be respected.

3. Further colonization of the Americas by European powers was prohibited.

4. Any European attempt to control or influence nations in the Western Hemisphere would be considered a hostile act against the U.S.

A staunch critic of the Mexican-American War, John Quincy Adams's final act of defiance came on February 21, 1848. As the House of Representatives prepared to honor U.S. Army officers involved in the conflict, Adams, in a moment of intense opposition, cried out "No!" Moments later, he collapsed from a massive cerebral hemorrhage. He passed away two days later in the Speaker's Room, marking a somber first - the first death within the Capitol Building. A young Abraham Lincoln, then a freshman representative, witnessed this historic event and even served as a pallbearer at Adams' funeral.

Charles Adams (Charlie)

29 May 1770 - 30 November 1800

Charles Francis Adams by Charles Bird King.

Charles, despite graduating from Harvard and passing the bar in 1792, struggled to establish a successful legal career. Married with two daughters, he battled alcoholism and infidelity, leading to estrangement from his father. Tragically, he died in New York City at the young age of 30 due to cirrhosis of the liver, becoming the first child of a sitting president to pass away.

Thomas Boylston Adams (Tommy)

15 September 1772 - 13 March 1832

Thomas Boylston Adams (1772-1832) by Charles Knight

Thomas, a Harvard graduate and lawyer, served as his brother John Quincy's secretary in the Netherlands and Prussia. Settling in Quincy, Massachusetts, he had a large family and briefly served in the state legislature. Recognized for his accomplishments, he was elected a Fellow of the American Academy of Arts and Sciences and later appointed a chief justice. However, like his brother Charles, Thomas struggled with alcoholism.

Elihu Adams

29 May 1741 – 10 August 1775

Elihu, the youngest brother of John Adams and uncle to John Quincy Adams, served his country during the American Revolution as a Captain in the Continental Army, leading troops against the British in Boston Harbor. Sadly, he passed away at the young age of 34 due to dysentery.

THE ADAMS NATIONAL HISTORICAL PARK

In 1776, the Adams family resided in Braintree, Massachusetts. A portion of Braintree was later incorporated as a separate town in 1792, named Quincy in honor of John Quincy Adams's great-grandfather and Abigail Adams's grandfather, John Quincy.

Should your travels ever bring you to Quincy, Massachusetts, consider making time for a visit to Adams National Historical Park. This historic site offers the opportunity to explore the birthplaces of both John and John Quincy Adams, and their later, grander residence known as Peacefield, which houses the unique stone library. However, it's always wise to confirm tour schedules and operating hours before heading out.

John Adams Birthplace (right) and John Quincy Adams Birthplace (left), Oil painting by G.N. Frankenstein, 1849., Courtesy of the Adams National Historical Park Service.

Georgius Agricola / Georg Pawer / Georg Bauer

24 March 1494 – 21 November 1555.

He is known as the father of mineralogy and the founder of geology.

Georgius Agricola, De re metallica, 1556

Audie Leon Murphy

20 June 1925 – 28 May 1971

Audie Murphy stands as a true American hero, recognized as the most decorated American soldier for hand-to-hand combat in World War II. Eager to fight against Germany, he attempted to enlist at

Audie Leon Murphy, JOOINN.com

the young age of sixteen, but was rejected by the Navy and Marines due to his age and weight. Determined, he altered his birthdate to meet the Army's requirements and successfully joined their ranks on June 30, 1942, just ten days after his seventeenth birthday.

Audie Murphy's bravery was recognized with every American combat award for valor available during his service, including the esteemed Medal of Honor. His courage also earned him accolades from France and Belgium. Additionally, in a long-overdue tribute, his home state of

Texas awarded him the Texas Legislative Medal of Honor on October 29, 2013.

Upon his discharge in 1945 at the war's end, Audie Murphy grappled with the effects of "battle fatigue," which we now recognize as Post-Traumatic Stress Disorder (PTSD). Despite his own struggles, he courageously became an advocate for veterans suffering from PTSD, highlighting the importance of treatment and support for those who had served their country.

Following his military service, Audie Murphy transitioned into a career in acting. He embarked on a successful path, starring in a variety of films and even securing a role in a television show. His experiences in the war undoubtedly influenced his performances, adding depth and authenticity to his portrayals.

Despite being eligible for a headstone marking his prestigious Medal of Honor status, Audie Murphy, in his characteristic humility, requested a simple headstone akin to that of a common soldier before his passing. Since the military adheres strictly to official records when inscribing headstones, Audie's tombstone bears his falsified birth year of 1924, a poignant reminder of his determination to serve his country even at a young age.

Tragically, Audie Murphy's life was cut short at the young age of forty-five in a plane crash in 1971.

His untimely death marked the end of a remarkable journey, from a determined young soldier to a celebrated war hero and accomplished actor. His legacy, however, lives on, inspiring generations with his bravery, humility, and unwavering dedication to his country.

Despite his humble request, Audie Murphy's gravesite has become the second most visited in Arlington National Cemetery, surpassed only by that of President John F. Kennedy.

This serves as a testament to the enduring admiration for this remarkable man, whose life continues to inspire even after his tragic passing.

Robert Lewis Howard

11 July 1939 – 23 December 2009

Colonel Robert Howard, a distinguished member of the United States Army Special Forces during the Vietnam War, holds the record as its most decorated officer and a recipient of the esteemed Medal

Robert Lewis Howard,
Courtesy of the Howard family.

of Honor. His exceptional bravery and unparalleled service have led many to consider him the most decorated service member in the history of the United States military.

Colonel Howard's exceptional bravery was recognized with three nominations for the Medal of Honor within a mere thirteen months. However, two of these acts of valor

Richard Nixon awarding the Medal of Honor to Robert Lewis Howard, Courtesy of the Howard family.

occurred during covert U.S. operations in Cambodia, resulting in him being awarded the Distinguished Service Cross and the Silver Star instead. His third nomination, for extraordinary heroism displayed on December 30, 1968, finally earned him the Medal of Honor, which he received from President Richard Nixon on March 24, 1971.

The Purple Heart, a poignant symbol of sacrifice, is bestowed upon those wounded or killed in service to their nation on or after April 5, 1917. It stands as the oldest military decoration still presented to members of the U.S. Armed Forces. Colonel Robert Howard, a testament to extraordinary resilience and humility, was awarded an impressive eight Purple Hearts. However, his true valor shines even brighter considering he was wounded a total of fourteen times. On six occasions, he modestly dismissed the severity of his injuries, deeming them insufficient to merit the Purple Heart.

The Bronze Star, another testament to valor and service, is awarded for heroic achievement or meritorious service in a combat zone. Colonel Howard's exceptional performance earned him four Bronze Stars, further highlighting his remarkable contributions during the Vietnam War.

Colonel Robert L. Howard's valor and dedication earned him a truly staggering number of military decorations and awards, too numerous to fully detail here.

I strongly encourage you to research his extraordinary service record; even the fictional heroics of Iron Man pale in comparison to this real-life American hero.

★

THE MEDAL OF HONOR

The Medal of Honor, the pinnacle of military recognition in the United States, is bestowed solely upon those who display unparalleled bravery and selflessness in the face of combat. Since its inception in 1861, over 3,400 individuals have been honored with this prestigious award. Reserved for members of the Armed Forces who perform acts of valor far exceeding the expectations of their duty, often at great personal risk, the Medal of Honor is a symbol of extraordinary courage and sacrifice. It is customarily presented by the President, acting on behalf of Congress, as a tribute to the recipient's exceptional heroism.

This esteemed award is not bestowed easily; recipients must have their acts of valor thoroughly documented and confirmed. To learn about the real-life heroes whose bravery eclipses even that of fictional characters like Superman, explore the website of the Congressional Medal of Honor Society (cmohs.org).

The following are three more Medal of Honor recipients that I feel are worth mentioning.

Dr. Mary Edwards Walker

26 November 1832 – 21 February 1919

Dr. Mary Edwards Walker, the sole female recipient of the Medal of Honor, was a Civil War surgeon known for crossing enemy lines to treat civilians. Captured as a suspected spy in 1864 while caring for a patient, she endured over four months as a prisoner of war. Following the conflict, President Andrew Johnson bestowed upon her the Medal of Honor. A trailblazer in a male-dominated era, Dr. Walker lived her life authentically, defying societal norms.

William "Willie" Johnson

12 July 1850 - 16 September 1941

William "Willie" Johnson holds the distinction of being the youngest-ever recipient of the Medal of Honor. He earned this esteemed recognition for his actions during the Civil War at the tender age of eleven, shortly before his twelfth birthday. The medal was officially bestowed upon him six weeks after he turned thirteen.

Jacklyn "Jack" Lucas

28 February 1928 - 5 June 2008

Jacklyn "Jack" Lucas, a World War II hero, followed in Audie Murphy's footsteps by enlisting in the Marine Corps at 14 after forging his mother's signature. At Iwo Jima, just five days after his 17th birthday, he selflessly threw himself on two grenades to protect his comrades. This act of valor earned him the Medal of Honor, making him the youngest recipient in the 20th century.

THE THEIA HYPOTHESIS

The Theia hypothesis proposes that a hypothetical planet named Theia collided with Earth approximately 4.5 billion years ago. The resulting debris from this massive impact eventually coalesced to create our moon. This hypothesis also offers an explanation for the Earth's unusually large core: Theia's core and mantle likely merged with Earth's during the collision.

— ★ —

HISTORICAL SITES & POINTS OF INTEREST IN THE FREEHOLD AREA

Monmouth Battlefield State Park

16 Business Route 33, Manalapan.

Walk the hallowed grounds where the Battle of Monmouth unfolded in 1778, a pivotal moment in the American Revolution. It consists of 1,818 acres of hills, orchards, woods, fields, and wetlands where the Battle of Monmouth Courthouse, the longest continuous battle of the Revolutionary War, was fought on June 28, 1778.

Located on Comb's Hill, the former command post of the Continental Army's artillery, the visitor center offers a wealth of information, artifacts unearthed from the battlefield, and a gift shop. The park itself boasts hiking and horseback riding trails, picnic spots, and a playground for children.

For information on events you may go to http://friendsofmonmouth.org.

Sutfin House*

Located on Route 522 (Englishtown - Freehold Road), Manalapan.

Jacob Sutfin built the house after buying the property in 1718. Six decades later, it found itself caught in the crossfire of the Battle of Monmouth. While it suffered some damage from musket fire, it was spared from cannonball impacts because the troops were aiming their cannons over the house in an attempt to reach their adversaries.

Craig House

198 Schibanoff Rd, Freehold.

John Craig, Sr., and his wife Ursula, originally from Scotland, settled in this area in 1685. Around 1710, he constructed the house that would become their family home.

Fast forward to 1778, during the Revolutionary War. John Jr. was away serving in the militia, leaving his wife Ann at home with their children. As the Battle of Monmouth approached, Ann realized their house would be in the thick of it. In a clever move, she hid the family silver at the bottom of their well and fled with her children to Upper Freehold, seeking safety away from the impending battle.

The British troops, upon occupying the empty house, turned it into a makeshift hospital. The sweltering heat drove the soldiers to drink heavily from the well, nearly emptying it. In doing so, they inadvertently discovered Ann Craig's hidden silver, which they promptly confiscated.

Freehold Raceway—a historic landmark as the oldest continuously operating racetrack in the United States. Harness racing events have been held at this location since the 1830s, but unfortunately, December 28, 2024, marked the final day of racing operations at Freehold Raceway.

Old Tennent Church

50 Tennent Road, Tennent.

Established in 1692 as a humble log cabin, the church served the community until 1731, when a more substantial structure was erected at its current location. This building, too, eventually proved inadequate and was replaced in 1751 with the present sanctuary, making it the oldest continuously used building in the area today.

A mere 27 years old when the Battle of Monmouth raged on June 28, 1778, the church was transformed into a makeshift hospital for wounded American soldiers. Physical reminders of that fateful day remain, including bloodstains and surgeon's marks on some pews. Legend has it that the blood belongs to Captain Henry Fauntleroy, who was struck by a cannonball while resting on a tombstone. The impact shattered the stone, and the mortally wounded captain was carried into the church, where he tragically passed away on his 22nd birthday.

The church grounds also serve as the final resting place for an unknown number of American and British soldiers, laid to rest in a shared grave. A memorial stone honors these unidentified fallen heroes, bearing the inscription: "Site of a common grave for unknown soldiers who fell at Monmouth June 28th 1778 Known only to God." Additionally, more than 250 recognized Revolutionary War veterans are interred here.

Upon entering the cemetery, make the second left and pause. To your right, you'll notice a distinct gap between the burial plots - a stretch of land devoid of tombstones. This ten-foot-wide path running along this section marks the very route Washington and his troops took to reach Perrine's Hill.

Old Tennent Church remains active, holding worship services, Sunday School, and Adult Bible Study. Reverend Doug Hughes, who served as the church's 21st pastor during my visit in 2020, joined the congregation in 2015. He has since retired from pastoral duties, and the church is currently in the process of selecting a new pastor.

The American Hotel

18-20 East Main Street, Freehold.

Constructed in 1824 as a stagecoach stop in the heart of town, the hotel underwent a transformation in the 1840s. It was demolished and rebuilt into a larger inn and tavern to cater to the growing number of travelers passing through Freehold Courthouse village on their way to the county seat. Notably, Abraham Lincoln stayed here in February 1861 during his journey to the White House.

The Hall of Records, the original courthouse
One East Main Street, Freehold.

Freehold itself was established in 1693 through legislation as one of Monmouth County's three founding townships. To ensure Freehold's status as the county seat, John Reid generously sold the land for the courthouse at a reduced price on August 26, 1714.

Construction of the first courthouse and jail on the Reid property commenced swiftly after the sale. Believed to be a modest wooden structure, it was replaced in 1719 following the escape of two prisoners. The second courthouse, however, only stood for eight years before succumbing to a fire in 1727. A new courthouse was built in 1731, and it was this very building where the Declaration of Independence was read aloud to the townspeople in 1776, just days after its adoption in Philadelphia.

The courthouse also served as a makeshift hospital for wounded British and American soldiers after the Battle of Monmouth. When General Henry Clinton retreated with his British forces under cover of night, approximately five wounded officers and 40 soldiers were left behind in the courthouse.

In 1806, construction started on a fourth courthouse, which was finished in 1809. This building stood until 1855, when it was severely damaged by a fire set by a female inmate in the county jail. After being rebuilt, the courthouse was ravaged by another fire in 1873. Yet again, they rebuilt, and ten years later, in 1874, an addition was constructed at the back of the courthouse, which now faces Court Street.

The courthouse faced yet another fire in 1930, but fortunately, this time the damage was limited to the stairway and belfry. The repairs were completed swiftly, in just four months.

For over two centuries, the county courthouse stood proudly at the intersection of Main and Court Streets, the very land purchased from John Reid. However, in 1954, a new courthouse was built two blocks north, adjacent to Monument Park on Court Street. The original courthouse, situated at the corner of Main and Court Streets, was then repurposed as the Hall of Records.

Interestingly, John Reid included a clause in the land sale to Monmouth County stipulating that if the property ceased to function as a courthouse, ownership would revert to the Reid family. Despite its current use as the Hall of Records, the building still houses a functioning courtroom, ensuring the fulfillment of Reid's condition.

Battle of Monmouth Statue

71 Monument Street, Freehold.

The monument stands as a lasting tribute to those who fought in the Battle of Monmouth Courthouse, marking the spot where General Lee fired the first shot that ignited the conflict on June 28, 1778. While the battle raged primarily between Monmouth Courthouse and Old Tennent Church, this monument serves as a poignant reminder of its beginning.

The monument's original statue, Liberty Triumphant, was unfortunately damaged by lightning in 1894 and subsequently replaced two years later.

In 1984, a rededication ceremony was held for the Battle of Monmouth Monument, and a time capsule was buried near the intersection of Court Street and Monument Street. The capsule is set to be opened in 2084, offering future generations a glimpse into the past and the legacy of those who fought in the battle.

Columbia Triumphant Park
Main Street, Freehold

You'll find a remnant of history: the top portion of the original monument that once graced the front of the current courthouse on Monument Street. This very piece was struck by lightning on August 15, 1894, marking a significant moment in the statue's story.

Covenhoven House (British General Clinton's Headquarters)
150 Main Street, Freehold.

Constructed in 1752-53, the home of the widowed Mrs. Covenhoven served as the headquarters for British General Henry Clinton and his officers just before the Battle of Monmouth. The house is positioned with its back to the street because, at the time of its construction, the street was only a few hundred feet away from the front of the house. In the early 1800s, Main Street was realigned to provide easier access to Mount Holly, resulting in the house's unusual orientation.

St. Peter's Episcopal Church

33 Throckmorton Street, Freehold.

Construction on this site began in 1771, but the social and economic disruptions of the Revolutionary War brought progress to a standstill. The building's frame was complete and enclosed at the time of the Battle of Monmouth. It's believed that wounded British soldiers were treated at St. Peter's before their covert journey to Sandy Hook. Later, it functioned as a storehouse for the Provincial Army. Building efforts resumed in 1792, culminating in its opening for worship in 1797. Today, it holds the distinction of being the oldest structure in continuous use within downtown Freehold.

Elks Point

At the convergence of East Main Street and Route 79 in Freehold, stands a poignant memorial dedicated to all Freehold residents who made the ultimate sacrifice while serving their country in times of war. Additionally, a separate memorial honors those brave residents who fought in World War II.

Bethel African Methodist Episcopal Cemetery
Old Monmouth Road, Freehold.

This cemetery, a resting place for nearly three dozen Black men who fought bravely to end slavery in the American Civil War, has sadly been overlooked and forgotten for many years. The Bethel AME Church, which owns the land, is now striving to have this sacred ground officially recognized as a military cemetery. It's a cause I wholeheartedly support; these men deserve to be remembered and honored for their courageous service and sacrifice.

The Freehold Grill
59 East Main Street, Freehold.

This beloved diner has been an integral part of the Freehold community since its doors first opened in 1947.

Freehold Public Library
28 1/2 East Main Street, Freehold.

The Freehold Public Library, generously funded by industrialist Andrew Carnegie, has been serving the community without interruption since 1904.

Sabrina the Teenage Witch's House

64 East Main Street, Freehold.

The house that famously served as the exterior for the fictional Spellman residence in the TV series *Sabrina the Teenage Witch* from 1996 to 2003 is located just across the street from Elks Point.

Federici's Family Restaurant

14 East Main Street, Freehold.

Spanning four generations, the Federici family has been delighting patrons with their authentic Italian cuisine and renowned thin crust pizza since 1921, a testament to their enduring legacy.

Sandy Hook Lighthouse

84 Mercer Road, Highlands.

The Sandy Hook Lighthouse, initially illuminated on June 11, 1764, served as a beacon for mariners navigating the New York Harbor. Built 500 feet from Sandy Hook's tip, the lighthouse now stands 1.5 miles away due to the northward push of sand by the longshore current over time.

During the Revolutionary War, the British seized control of the lighthouse from 1776 until the war's end in 1783. Following the Battle of Monmouth, General Clinton and his troops made a clandestine retreat under the cover of night to Sandy Hook, where they crossed over to New York.

The Sandy Hook Lighthouse holds the unique distinction of being a National Historic Landmark within another National Historic Landmark. It boasts its own National Historic Landmark status and is also a part of the larger Fort Hancock and Sandy Hook Proving Ground Historic District National Historic Landmark.

Village Inn
Main and Water Streets, Englishtown.

Constructed in 1726, the Village Inn, then known as the Herbert Inn after its early owner Daniel Herbert, played a significant role in American history. It served as General Washington's headquarters in the immediate aftermath of the Battle of Monmouth, on June 29-30. Notably, it was within these walls that a pivotal exchange of letters between Washington and General Charles Lee transpired, ultimately resulting in Lee's arrest and subsequent court-martial.

Laird's Applejack
One Laird Road, Scobeyville.

Laird & Company, the leading producer of applejack and apple brandy, holds the distinction of being the oldest continuously operating distillery in the United States. Its roots trace back to around 1698 when William Laird, a Scotsman, settled in Monmouth County and began distilling the plentiful local apple crop.

Even George Washington was a fan of Laird's products during the Colonial era, requesting and receiving the recipe for "cyder spirits." In 1780, just four years after American independence and two years after the Battle of Monmouth, Laird's was granted the nation's first distillery permit. This federal license to produce apple brandy for medicinal purposes proved crucial, likely saving the company from ruin during Prohibition.

Today, Laird & Company remains a thriving family business, now managed by the eighth, ninth, and tenth generations of the Laird family. This remarkable longevity is a testament to the quality of their products and the enduring strength of their family bond. Few companies can boast such a rich history, and the fact that Laird's has been family-run for over 300 years speaks volumes about their dedication and resilience.

Oakley Farm

189 Wemrock Road, Freehold.

This farm's origins trace back to 1686, when the British Crown and the Proprietors of East Jersey sold the land to John Barclay. The following year, John transferred 500 acres to Robert Barclay. Subsequently, the property changed hands multiple times, passing through nine different owners until it was inherited by Elizabeth Oakley. In recognition of its historical significance, the farm was listed on the National Register of Historic Places in 1994.

Freehold Townships historical Toll House

189 Wemrock Road, Freehold.

On the Oakley farm, there's a small red building that once served as a toll house. It housed a toll collector who charged travelers for using the dirt road. This toll system helped the local farmers maintain the road, with the toll houses owned and operated by a group of farmers living along it. The fees were modest: $.05 for a single horse and $.10 for a team of two. Those who chose not to pay had to take the unmaintained road, risking broken wheels or injuries to their horses.

West Freehold Schoolhouse

209 Wemrock Road, Freehold.

This school served the community continuously from 1847 until 1936, when it was closed due to the consolidation of school districts within Freehold Township.

Jersey Freeze

120 Manalapan Avenue, Freehold.

This beloved ice cream shop, founded by the Blackmore family in 1952, has been a cherished tradition in

Freehold for generations. Be sure to indulge in their iconic black and white milkshakes!

And lastly, I know some of my homies would be in a tizzy if I didn't mention **Bruce Springsteen.** He's from my hometown too. If you want to check out where he lived, here are the addresses:

87 Randolph Street. It was torn down and is now the driveway entrance to the parking lot of St. Rose of Lima. (Lee-muh, not lima beans as Sr. Mary Kennedy, my sixth grade teacher, always said.) It was the home of his grandparents and where he once lived.

39 ½ Institute Street and 68 South Street: These addresses are where Springsteen lived at different points. Please remember that these are private residences now, so be respectful of the current occupants and their property. No trespassing or disturbing the peace!

BATTLE OF MONMOUTH

Many became heroes on June 28, 1778, during the Battle of Monmouth. The following is a little information about just two of the ordinary people that had their lives changed on that day. Whenever people go to war (no matter when or where), those people will be forever changed.

The Battle of Monmouth saw many rise to the occasion, becoming heroes in the midst of conflict. Among them were ordinary individuals whose lives were irrevocably altered that day. Mary Ludwig Hays, a civilian accompanying her husband in the Pennsylvania Artillery, and Solomon Parsons, a young soldier from Massachusetts simply obeying orders, exemplify how war, regardless of time or place, leaves an indelible mark on those who experience it.

Mary Ludwig Hays

1754-1832

During the Revolutionary War, it wasn't unusual for wives to follow their husbands into battle, and Mary Ludwig Hays was no exception. On the scorching, humid battlefield of June 28, 1778, heatstroke claimed many lives alongside musket and cannon fire. Mary, nicknamed "Molly," tirelessly tended to the wounded and ferried pitchers of water to the soldiers and cannons. The men would shout "Molly! Pitcher!" when they needed her, and thus, the legendary name "Molly Pitcher" was born.

When her husband, William, collapsed and was removed from the field, Molly didn't miss a beat. She stepped into his position at the cannon, swabbing and loading it. A musket ball or cannonball even tore through her skirt, to which she reportedly quipped, "Well, that could have been worse," and carried on with her duties.

The men of the Pennsylvania Artillery often described Molly as a "twenty-two-year-old illiterate pregnant woman who smoked and chewed tobacco and swore as well as any of the male soldiers."

Her courage under fire earned her the respect of the troops, and George Washington himself inquired about the brave woman he'd seen manning the cannons. In recognition of her service, he promoted her as a non-commissioned officer, earning her the nickname "Sergeant Molly" for the rest of her life. In 1822, Pennsylvania awarded Molly an annual pension of $40 for her wartime contributions.

Solomon Parsons

1757 - 1831

Solomon was just a twenty-one-year-old kid from Massachusetts when General Washington encountered General Lee's troops retreating from the British. Furious at Lee's ineptitude, Washington took charge. With the main part of his army still distant and the British approaching, Washington had to act quickly. He ordered a group of men to move forward into a "Point of Woods" to delay the British moving forward. Solomon was one of those picked to go on this mission.

He got off three shots before being forced to retreat. Solomon later recounted, "I turned left and saw the enemy had outflanked our men who were exposed outside the woods. I ran a short distance, but the enemy fired on me. One bullet hit my heel, severely wounding me. The next volley broke my thigh." Overwhelmed, he was bayoneted and beaten before being left for dead in the sweltering heat, robbed of his possessions.

After seven grueling hours, he was discovered clinging to life and transported back to the makeshift field hospital at the Tennent Meeting House (Old Tennent Church).

Solomon Parsons survived until 1831. On his tombstone the inscription reads: "suffering 53 years from a wound received at Monmouth Battle, where he bled for his Country. Reader, pause, recollect what it cost to gain your liberty."

Let me just reiterate what the last sentence on Solomon's tombstone reads:

**Reader, pause, recollect what
it cost to gain your liberty.**

─────── ★ ───────

THE SUTFIN HOUSE

*The Sutfin House, the oldest building within Monmouth Battlefield State Park, has silently observed some of the Revolution's most pivotal moments. Built over 300 years ago by Jacob Sutfin after he acquired the land in 1718, the house has evolved over time. Thanks to expansions in the 1820s and 1840s, it now stands as a two-and-a-half-story structure.

During the Battle of Monmouth on June 28, 1778, the Sutfin family found their home right in the heart of the conflict. The farmhouse was caught in the crossfire of the largest artillery exchange of the American Revolution, a fact

The Sutfin House from Exploring Photography with Joe Valencia, joevalenciaphotography.blogspot.com, valencia32photo@gmail.com

documented in battle maps and historical accounts. One of the most intense and well-recorded clashes occurred in the Sutfin's apple orchard and along its fences. Adding to the drama, Derick Sutfin's sons were part of the militia and, on the eve of the battle, at least one of them participated in the capture of fifteen British soldiers caught off guard while doing their laundry.

Beyond its historical value as a preserved early 18th-century Dutch farmhouse, the Sutfin House is crucial for understanding the dynamic shifts of the Battle of Monmouth. The cider orchard behind the house initially served as a strategic point for the British army's right flank. As the battle progressed, it became the site of the Continental Army's counteroffensive.

Monmouth Battlefield is hallowed ground where men and women fought and died, their blood soaking within the soil here, in pursuit of America's freedom from British rule. Preserving this house serves as a tribute not only to the significance of this historical event but also to the memory of those courageous individuals who sacrificed their lives there.

The Sutfin House was put on the endangered list in 2020. If you would like to help preserve this important part of America's history, please go to **http://spot.fund/ TheRestorationOfSutfinHouse.** Outside grants, raising funds, and even just awareness of the needs of a historic site can be monumental in saving them.

I feel that the preservation of this house is so important that part of the proceeds of this book will be donated to the restoration and preservation of Sutfin House.

ACKNOWLEDGEMENTS

To my beta readers, the brave souls who dared to venture into the uncharted territory of my manuscript, thank you! Your feedback was both honest and insightful.

I appreciate your willingness to go on this adventure with me.

Dublin Avestro

Cassidy Gusera

Ruth Harper

Julia Young

SPECIAL ACKNOWLEDGEMENTS

Courtney Lopez—

My keen-eyed junior editor and biggest fan.

Jay Lopez—

My oracle of the arcane and fantastical.

Your help, encouragement, and unwavering support have meant the world to me throughout this journey. You are both cherished beyond measure.

http://spot.fund/TheRestorationOfSutfinHouse